THISTLE HILL

A SUSPENSE NOVEL

RICK CHARLEBOIS

THISTLE HILL
Copyright © 2017 by Rick Charlebois

Scriptures taken from the Holy Bible, New International Version®, NIV®. Copyright © 1973, 1978, 1984, 2011 by Biblica, Inc.™ Used by permission of Zondervan. All rights reserved worldwide. www.zondervan.com The "NIV" and "New International Version" are trademarks registered in the United States Patent and Trademark Office by Biblica, Inc.™

Printed in Canada

ISBN: 978-1-4866-1336-6

Word Alive Press
131 Cordite Road, Winnipeg, MB R3W 1S1
www.wordalivepress.ca

MIX
Paper from
responsible sources
FSC® C103567

Library and Archives Canada Cataloguing in Publication

Charlebois, Rick, author
    Thistle Hill / Rick Charlebois.

Issued in print and electronic formats.
ISBN 978-1-4866-1336-6 (softcover).--ISBN 978-1-4866-1337-3
(ebook)

    I. Title.

PS8605.H36897T45 2017   C813'.6   C2017-900042-X
                                                C2017-900043-8

SUSAN LEFT HER WORKPLACE, THE BUGLER PUB, TIRED BUT PLEASED that it had been a good night for tips. Her feet ached from the busy eight-hour-shift she'd just completed.

Her long slender legs carried her quickly across the empty parking lot as she pulled her collar up around her neck and walked into the cool, mist-filled night. Inhaling deeply, she chased away the stale pub air from her lungs. She walked along the street, the moon peeking out from behind clouds then quickly retreating, leaving her in darkness. Few people were on the street at this hour.

Susan replayed the news reports she'd heard on the radio concerning attacks on women; the police had warned women to avoid walking alone. The hair on the back of her neck stood up as she glanced to her left and right, even behind, trepidation flooding her senses. Although nothing appeared to suggest any danger, she couldn't shed the feeling of being followed.

Starting down the subway stairs, her fear intensified. But still, she saw nothing that should make her feel uncomfortable.

Boarding the subway, she headed for home. Two other women shared the subway car; like her, they appeared to be on their way home from work. To her right, several seats away, a man with a wild beard and ratty clothes was enjoying a deep sleep. His robust snores, although somewhat annoying, almost made her laugh.

Over the top of the door, she caught sight of an automobile advertisement. Susan dreamed of the day when she could afford a car and not have to make this nightly trip.

Susan began to unwind as the familiarity of her surroundings eased her tension. The rhythm of the wheels rolling over the tracks almost put her to sleep. Her head bobbed and suddenly dropped with such force that it awakened her. She sat up straight to avoid falling to sleep. Before long, her stop was announced. It was time to disembark, time to start the last leg of the journey home.

She climbed to street level. As her condo building was now only a few short blocks away, she set aside her fear and admonished herself for acting like a child. When she had been a little girl, she had often called to Dad to check for monsters under the bed. He'd always assured everything was all right—and it always was.

Arriving home and passing through the secure entrance calmed her nerves. The feeling of safety intensified as the door closed behind her. After a short elevator ride, she reached her unit, unlocked the door, and breathed a sigh of relief.

Suddenly, a strong force pushed her through the door. A gloved hand covered her mouth and held a knife against her throat. The knife pressed hard against her skin and cut through. She felt warm blood trickling down her neck. As the pressure of the knife eased, an injection pierced her arm. Within seconds, she had lost her will to struggle and was trapped in a paralyzed body.

As the intruder picked her up, she saw for the first time her attacker's elderly face. He carried her to the bedroom and placed her on the bed. Her attacker's lips moved, but she couldn't discern his words. There was no connection between her mind and body. Who was this man and why was he doing this to her?

Removing all his clothes, including the gray-haired wig and false beard he had used to disguise himself, he placed everything in a plastic bag, walked over to the bed, and looked down at Susan.

She is a cancer in my life, he thought, knowing that he had to cut her out. *Why does it always have to end this way?*

He was desperate to find someone who would be faithful to him, who wouldn't flirt and carry on with other men. Tragically, the women in his life always ended up abandoning him or playing him for a fool.

He had been abandoned at birth and had no recollection of ever being held in the loving arms of a mother. From birth to eighteen years old, he had been a ward of the Child Welfare Agency. Although there had been foster parents, they had always rejected him and sent him back.

Once, when he'd been fourteen years old, he had fallen in love with a girl housed in the same facility. But she dumped him for an older boy.

When he was old enough to be sent out on his own, he had several relationships with co-workers, but they always ended up cheating on him. He had learned he could never trust a woman. For his own protection, he knew he had to be sure he was always the one in control; if a relationship had to end, it would be his decision, not hers.

An hour later he left the bedroom, his expression revealing nothing of the gruesome rape and murder that had just taken place.

He wiped the blood from his knife and headed for the bathroom. He showered, making sure to remove any blood that had splashed on him. He thoroughly cleaned the shower, then stepped out and took his clothes from the plastic bag.

I will not despair, he thought as he dressed. *I know there is a woman out there for me.*

He went to the refrigerator, found the fixings for a sandwich, grabbed a beer, and enjoyed a late-night snack. Once he had finished eating, he meticulously cleaned the kitchen and reapplied his disguise. He took the collapsible white cane and tinted eyeglasses from his jacket pocket and gathered his rubber gloves. He poked his head into the bedroom and bid his victim adieu.

Off he went into the early morning, making his way home. His white cane tapped its way along the sidewalk, telegraphing the mystery of his secrets. He knew that ending it with Susan had been the right thing to do. There would soon be a new relationship to foster, and maybe it would be the one—the woman he'd waited for all his life, the one who would be true to him.

He smiled as he watched those he encountered move in a wide arc around him. They looked at him as if they thought they might catch his blindness. Few people ever spoke to him or even acknowledged his presence.

When he reached the bus stop, he tapped up the pole holding the sign and headed toward the bench. He could hardly keep from laughing as he watched the commuters scatter to make room for him.

The bus rumbled up to the stop and once again he was given priority by this very polite crowd. An elderly woman gave up her seat for him, which he gratefully accepted. He was impressed by their kindness this particular morning; he had travelled using this disguise other times and hadn't been given this kind of consideration. He wondered if people had more compassion because of the early hour. Maybe people were so worn down by the evening that they had nothing left to give.

The bus driver announced his stop and he disembarked. He went to the neighborhood park's washroom and entered a stall to remove his disguise and return to his real self, Dennis Cain.

As Dennis exited the washroom, his eyes took some time to adjust to the bright sunshine. He joyfully watched children playing in the park and thought how much he would like to be a father. He was eager to start a new search for his special women. Who would she be?

CHAPTER TWO

DAVID MACDONALD, OWNER AND CEO OF STAR INVESTMENTS, WAS eager to end his workday and head home. Tired from the day's stress, he walked across the parking lot, his bald head glistening in the sun. His broad shoulders drooped and his steps lacked energy. Even the sight of his beloved Porsche failed to lift his spirits. Of late, his life seemed so pointless.

He pulled out of the parking lot and into the stop-and-go city traffic he dealt with day after day.

Finally he came to the ramp where he merged onto the highway. He was pleased that the traffic was moving well this night. As he got lost in the drive, his mind wandered to an article he had read in yesterday's paper. People had been asked, "What is the purpose of life? Do we keep going through the motions and at the end die and that's it? Or do we have some higher purpose?"

One of his friends had said, "Even if someone hasn't formally addressed this question, the way they live reveals what they believe. Some people try to cram as much into their lives as they can because they don't believe there is any afterlife. Others, who have deep convictions, are often willing to give up much in this life as an investment for the next. Still others don't even want to consider such things."

David realized that questions like these had been entering his consciousness more and more as he moved into the autumn of his life.

His thoughts were interrupted as a car collided with the guardrail and spun into the car next to it. David veered toward the guardrail and narrowly avoided a collision. As he looked in his rearview mirror, he realized he had barely missed being part of an accident. He was thankful to be ahead of the traffic jam the accident would cause. Although he felt guilt, his comfort held a higher place in his mind than the pain and suffering of those involved.

His guilt was short-lived. He went along his way as if nothing had happened.

He was impressed with how well his Porsche Boxster had responded. He took a deep breath to enjoy the smell of the leather interior, then reached for the radio knob to hush his mind with the incredible sound system. The radio was tuned to a report of another killing in downtown Toronto. The police weren't giving out many details, though they were warning women to be vigilant and not travel alone. Even though the police hadn't confirmed a connection between the various killings, the press had dubbed this to be the fourth victim of a serial killer.

David changed the station to let the soothing sounds of jazz unwind him. It wasn't long before he pulled up to the gated entry of his new home.

The large stone wall and wrought iron gate, accented with beautiful gardens, attested to the prosperity he and his wife Deborah had achieved. His business was very successful and Deborah was a judge.

As he parked beside his company car, a BMW 750LI, he wondered why, with everything he had, he still felt something was missing.

He entered his home through the side door that opened to the kitchen. Deborah was cutting vegetables for a salad. David walked up behind her and kissed the back of her neck.

"Ooh, that felt good," she said. "But I must tell you, my husband will be home any minute now."

They both laughed and Deborah asked him how his day had been. He went to the cupboard and reached for a wine glass. He asked her if she would like some wine as well.

"Yes, please."

David poured the wine and handed it to her. He walked to the other side of the island, pulled out a stool, and sat facing her. "I had quite a surprise today," he said as he took a sip.

Deborah stopped working and gave him an inquisitive look. "Don't keep me in suspense."

David put down his glass and leaned forward, placing his elbows on the island and joining his hands under his chin. "Edith told me she's going to retire at the end of the year."

Deborah's jaw dropped and her eyes widened. "Really?"

"That's what she said."

"Are there any health problems?"

"I don't think so."

Deborah tossed the salad fixings in a bowl and stirred in some dressing. "What are you going to do?"

David leaned back. "Well, I'm going to speak with her again tomorrow to make sure there's nothing wrong. After twenty years, I don't want to lose her over some misunderstanding. If it truly is her wish to retire, I'll have to hire someone to replace her. But enough about me. How was your day?"

Deborah's eyes sparkled and a smile of excitement brightened her face. "I too had some news today. I've been assigned a somewhat unusual case. The complainant is charging the defendant with age discrimination. With the impact the boomers are having on the workplace, and society in general, this case is on the cutting edge. My decision could impact the way seniors are treated in the future."

David placed his hands behind his head. "You know dear, those seniors of the future are us," he said with a silly grin on his face. "So I'm happy it's you hearing this case."

After dinner, Deborah kissed him goodbye and went off to something at church. David didn't ask exactly what; he really didn't want to know. He felt there was a wedge pushing them apart. It seemed to him that her interests had changed since she'd been "born again." If she wasn't curled up on the couch reading her Bible, she was going off to church meetings. These things took up too much of her time. He wasn't against her belonging to a church—as a boy he'd gone to church every Sunday with his dad—but he found it hard to understand why Deborah, with all her education and success, felt the need to be stimulated by religious rules, rituals, and teachings. He wondered how anyone could look at the events of the current day and believe there was an all-powerful and loving God behind it all. Such a God, if he existed, wouldn't allow the atrocities that happened every day. In fact, the worst of these atrocities were perpetrated by religious people who acted in the name of their God. He couldn't understand what Deborah got out of it. Whenever he tried to discuss it, it never ended well. It seemed to him their lives had diverged.

David remembered when they had first met, how they both loved the same kinds of music, the same foods, and had believed the same things. They had set goals and worked together to achieve them. Now everything was falling apart. He worried about where their lives were headed.

David decided to unpack the boxes left over from the recent move. As he did, he came across a writing he had clipped out of a book several years ago. He glanced at the author's name: Anonymous. He chuckled to himself. Must be Greek, with a name like that.

The article told the story of an elderly homebuilder who had decided to retire, but his employer had asked him to build one more house as a special favor. When he was done, the employer handed him the key and said, "This is my gift to you, to say thanks for all your years of good service." The builder was shocked and regretted that he had been so focused on retirement that he hadn't done his best work.

In life the choices you make today build the house you will live in to-morrow, he thought, remembering the article's closing line.

As David thought about this, he realized that he and Deborah had built wisely, for the most part. They were financially well off, but maybe they should have paid more attention to their relationship. Even though he had everything a person could ask for, he still wasn't happy. Perhaps he needed to think more about the purpose of his life.

It makes sense, he thought. *There must be a purpose to life or else it's all for naught.*

He had met many people during his life who had spent their lives doing something they hated, simply because it provided a desirable income. They usually weren't happy. Others, like his dad, had enjoyed their work even though it never produced great wealth; they experienced happy lives. David was envious of how much his dad had enjoyed life with what little he had.

David began to realize he had a problem, but he wasn't sure what it was. Was he depressed, having a midlife crisis? Or could it be he and Deborah had grown so far apart that they were no longer good for each other? He knew he had to face up to what he was feeling. The question was where to start.

When Deborah returned from church, David was sitting in the den. She walked over to him and gave him a kiss.

"So what have you been up to?" she asked.

"Not much. I did a little work and unpacked some of my boxes. How about you?"

Deborah sat in the chair across from him and smiled enthusiastically. "I met a man tonight. His name is Paul." She raised her eyebrows. "And guess what?"

"I've got no idea."

"He has an office in the same building as you!"

David shifted his weight and leaned forward. "Really? What's his business?"

"Well, he's a psychologist with his own practice, but he's also a minister."

David tilted his head. "Why does he work as a psychologist rather than a minister?"

"I don't know, but you can ask him yourself. I've invited Paul and his wife Mary to dinner next week. I think you'll like him, and I'm anxious to get to know Mary."

Great, David thought. *It's not enough that she's immersing herself in this religion stuff, now she's inviting a minister to our home.*

CHAPTER THREE

Diary Entry, June 12, 2012

Thought of the day: "No problem can be solved from the same level of consciousness that created it." (Albert Einstein)

It's been over a month since we moved into our new house and I've just finished unpacking the last of my books and music. My man cave is organized and ready to enjoy. I never dreamed I would own an 8,000-square-foot home with a gated entrance. Somehow it seems fate has made an error and moved me along life in someone else's path.

It doesn't seem that long ago when I was driving along the old country road with my dad, on our way to deliver his produce in Toronto. The road travelled through an enchanted forest, and as a child I enjoyed the rollercoaster excitement of dipping down into the valley and climbing back up the other side. Dad knew how to control the speed so I felt the maximum thrill in my stomach. We could see a private golf course from the road and it looked absolutely beautiful. It had well-manicured greens and the fairways rolled over gently undulating land accented with ponds and a babbling brook. The long winding entrance road and spectacular clubhouse suggested it was set aside for the elite. I was in awe of the estates along the way with names like

Hollyhock Way, Rose Bush Hill, and Dragonfly Lane. The homes were hidden in their own forests and rolling hills; their elaborate gates were decorated with beautiful flower gardens and land-scaping that suggested the loving care of master gardeners.

I wondered what kind of people would live in such a place, and now here I am, the proud owner of Thistle Hill.

Deborah and I chose the name carefully after doing some research. Since we had thistle on the grounds, we decided to dig up some information on it. Thistle was an ancient Celtic sym-bol of nobility of character as well as birth and it's been the national emblem of Scotland since the reign of Alexander III (1249–1286). According to a legend, an invading Norse army once attempted to sneak up at night upon a Scottish army's en-campment. During this operation, a barefoot Norseman had the misfortune to step upon a thistle, causing him to cry out in pain, thus alerting the Scots. Deborah also found that in medieval times it was thought thistle could return hair to bald heads. Well, that made it an ideal name pertaining to me and my heritage.

I wish my dad was still alive so he could see this property and share in my success. I can picture him looking over our land and house with eyes the size of quarters and with a worried look saying to me, in his thick Scottish accent, "Are you sure you can afford all this, Davy?"

Oh how I miss my dad! I can still vividly remember sitting on his lap, being held tightly in his loving arms and feeling so safe, so completely loved. It was a different world then. Things were less hectic, there were fewer choices to make, people took time to talk, and everything closed down on Sunday so families could spend time together.

Today I feel like I'm walking through a house of mirrors; you never know for sure which one is your real reflection. I'm expending so much energy trying to be everything everyone wants me to be. I'm tired; I don't even know who I am.

I wonder if it was like that in my dad's time. Have the times changed, or is this just the cost of growing up?

Well, it's time to start my day and join the rat race. I've heard it said the problem with the rat race is that even if you win, you're still a rat.

———

AS DAVID ENTERED THE OFFICE, HE LOOKED AROUND AT THE RECENT renovations. He was still surprised he had let an interior decorator run wild—and what surprised him even more is that he liked it.

The walls were a moss-green on a rough-textured surface. The bamboo floor was a light beechwood tone and the room was accented with strategically placed palm trees. The client chairs were arranged underneath the palm trees and had the unusual feature of being rocking chairs. Their color perfectly matched the earth tones of the receptionist's work area.

David smiled at his secretary. "Good morning, Edith. How are you today?"

Sitting very erect in her chair, her gray hair pulled tightly into a bun, she formed her lips into a small mandatory smile. "Fine, thank you. I have a few messages written down. In particular, Mr. Davies is anxious to speak with you." She handed him Mr. Davies' message first, then the others.

"Thanks. I'll call him right away." He started to walk away, and then turned. "Would you arrange your schedule so we could have a talk after your lunch today?"

A look of surprise fell over her face. "Would one o'clock be fine with you?"

"That would be great. Thank you."

The morning went by quickly. David went for a light lunch and made sure he was back in time to meet with Edith.

Ever so promptly, at the stroke of one o'clock, Edith tapped on his door.

"Come in," David said as he walked to the front of his large, old-fashioned oak desk. Behind him was a wall of windows that overlooked the city.

He invited Edith to take a seat on the couch. David pulled his chair so it was facing her. He sat with his fingers intertwined over his stomach and his elbows on the arms of the chair.

"I must say, Edith, you took me completely by surprise when you told me yesterday you intend to retire at the end of this year." A frown covered his forehead. "As I thought about it last night, I wondered if there were any particular issues we should be talking about?"

Edith tilted her head, looking perplexed. "Well, I will be sixty-five in November and sixty-five is the age when people retire."

David leaned back in his chair. "But is that what you want?"

"It's what I've been planning for,"

"So what are your retirement goals? Do you want to travel?"

Edith relaxed somewhat. "I haven't given much thought to that. I probably will travel, and maybe winter in Florida, but that's something I can decide once I'm retired. I don't want to be the family visitor who doesn't know when it's time to go."

"Edith, you are an incredibly valuable asset to this company. You're my right hand person. Don't feel for a moment you're not wanted here. Be sure your choice to retire is what you want, not what you think others want you to do. You don't need to retire simply because you're sixty-five years old." He smiled, leaning back in his chair. "Remember, you were the one who wrote the excellent speech I made for the Christian women's investment club. In it you noted that history is filled with the accomplishments of aged people. You cited that in biblical times, Abraham was called at the age of seventy-five and Moses was called at the age of eighty. In more recent times, England's Winston Churchill, Canada's Lester Pearson, and the United States' Abraham Lincoln all had their finest hour in their advanced years. Don't limit yourself or let anyone define you by your age."

He moved from his chair and sat beside her on the couch.

"I hope you won't take this discussion as an attempt by me to change your mind," he continued. "Only you can make that decision. I care for you and I want to be sure you're making it for the right reasons. So I ask you to give our discussion consideration and in a week or two let me know what you decide. If you still want to retire, I will respect your decision—and if you should decide you want to continue working here, nothing would make me happier." He gently took her hand in his. "Thank you, Edith, for all you do and how well you do it."

Her eyes watered. "Thank you, Mr. MacDonald," she said, a little choked up. "I'll think about what you've said and let you know in a couple of weeks." Edith withdrew her hand from his and regained her composure. "Will that be all, sir?"

"Yes. Thank you, Edith."

CHAPTER FOUR

As Deborah left for work, she popped in a CD Paul had given her to listen to.

"Time is the only true treasure we have," the speaker said. "Everything else is earned through investing our time. If we want to do well in life, we need to be very purposeful in how we invest our time." His presentation ended with a question: "How much time do you spend with those who are most important to you?"

This hit Deborah right between the eyes. She recognized she had been applying a great amount of time to her relationship with God, but perhaps her relationship with her husband was suffering because of it. It would be so much easier if she and David were of the same conviction when it came to religion. She recognized her need to pray and think more about how to balance her time better.

She pulled into her private parking space, keen to get her day started. The brief outlining the age discrimination case would be waiting on her desk. Excited as she was to get started, the beautiful gardens adorning the walkway to her office enticed her to stop and enjoy them. The gardens were a riot of color—bright red and yellow dahlias, black-eyed Susans, geraniums, and her personal favorite, the ever-beautiful roses. She stopped to smell the roses and complimented the gardener, who was busy keeping the beds tidy.

The courts were housed in a massive sandstone building constructed in the late 1800s. It had been designated a national historic site in 1965. The front of the building was dominated by dual towers and prominent round-arched openings. The use of materials originating from across Canada provided contrasting textures of stone in shades of russet and beige. Inside, visitors were greeted by impressive domed ceilings, stained-glass windows, and richly polished dark oak walls. On this particular morning, Deborah thought how appropriate it was to be working a case about ageism from such an historic building.

After the daily greetings and water-cooler topics had been exhausted with her secretary George, she was off to her office, eager to familiarize herself with the arguments of the case.

The plaintiff, Ms. Cate Curte, alleged that the owner of Starlight Nightclub had fired her because she was too old. Her exotic dancing career had started six years ago at the age of forty and she had worked throughout this time exclusively with Starlight. Ms. Curte had been blindsided when she was called into the owner's office and told that her services would no longer be required. There had been no previous indication of any problem, so the news had shocked her, but she had stood her ground and demanded an explanation. The boss had responded that he wanted to go in a new direction with younger girls.

The defendant claimed he intended to pursue a younger customer base and therefore required younger dancers. Even the décor was to be changed. Ms. Curte's termination had nothing to do with her age but was strictly the result of a new business plan focused on increased profits.

Deborah realized intense research would be needed to hear this case. Under the Ontario Human Rights Code, employers were barred from treating a worker differently because of their age. In this particular case, she wondered how that should be balanced with the owner's right to explore new markets. There was no indication that Ms. Curte's age had compromised her ability to do her job. Deborah wondered how age would affect audience response.

Some people were attracted to those who were older than they, which wasn't unusual in society, so was age truly a factor to Starlight's plan?

No similar cases on file had established a strong precedent. Indeed, Deborah would be blazing a new trail. Her preparation would need to focus on refreshing and updating her knowledge of the Human Rights Code.

CHAPTER FIVE

Diary Entry, January 15, 2013

Thought of the day: "What is worse: ignorance or apathy? I don't know and I don't care." (Jimmy Buffett, probably after a few drinks, in "Margaritaville.")

Deborah and I hosted a retirement party for Edith Bickle last night. We invited a few of our long-time clients who have dealt with Edith over the years and a few of her nearest and dearest friends. We had the meal catered by "Outdoor Gourmet." They presented a banquet to rival any of the finest restaurants, all prepared on a barbecue, along with a succulent assortment of fine wines. The guests were picked up by limousine so they could enjoy the evening without worrying about driving.

The party also allowed us to showcase our amazing new property and home. The view from our backyard goes on as far as the eye can see and the sunsets are spectacular. For our guests, it was their first time at the home. They all seemed to be very impressed with what they saw.

Throughout the evening, the atmosphere was enhanced by the soft caress of live music. He moved from rock-and-roll to western to quiet background music with an uncanny timing that had people singing one moment and then subtly drifting into quiet conversation the next.

We concluded the evening with the customary speeches and remembrances, wishing Edith a happy retirement. Our parting gift for Edith was an all-expense paid trip to China, a place I knew she had always wanted to visit.

Today will be the first day for my new secretary, Ms. Catherine Boudreau, to be on her own without Edith guiding her. This will be quite a change for me. Catherine is only twenty-six years old and could easily have been a model. Very much the opposite of Edith, she has a relaxed confidence that puts one at ease the minute you meet her. Although incredibly beautiful, she doesn't seem to know it. Catherine has already proven to be very capable and efficient.

———

WHEN DAVID ENTERED THE OFFICE, CATHERINE WASN'T AT HER DESK. He wondered if she would be as punctual as Edith always had been. The thought no sooner entered his mind than he saw Catherine exit his office.

Her smile lit up the room. "Good morning, sir. I have your messages and a coffee waiting for you on your desk."

"Thank you and good morning to you, too."

David entered his office and was impressed. His coffee was black, just as he liked it, and Catherine had placed his messages on his desk where he usually put them after Edith handed them to him. After all her years with him, Edith had never entered his office without being invited. Catherine's approach was much less formal, but David liked it.

Throughout the morning, Catherine remained a step ahead of him. She reminded him of Walter Eugene "Radar" O'Reilly from *M*A*S*H*. Just as he got ready to call her, she'd be there with exactly what he needed. It was almost uncanny.

As she sat in front of his desk to go over some details with him, he got lost looking into her deep blue eyes. He mentally scolded himself for being unprofessional. Once they had completed the tasks at hand, she thanked him for choosing to hire her and expressed her intention to do everything necessary to make sure he never regretted his decision.

He assured her that she was doing a fantastic job so far.

She reached across his desk and laid her hand on his. "You don't know how much I appreciate your words."

Then she turned and left the office. His eyes followed her out the door.

He was amazed with how fast the morning had gone. It was already slightly past his lunchtime. When he left for lunch, Catherine had already turned the phone over to the answering service and left. No doubt men were lined up to take her out for lunch; no sooner had that thought entered his mind than he realized she had never spoken about a boyfriend.

David decided to eat at a nearby deli known for their excellent corned beef sandwiches. As usual, the restaurant was extremely busy and he wondered if he would be able to find a seat. Suddenly, he heard his name being called and turned to see Catherine waving him to her table. He collected his sandwich and drink and approached her.

She flashed one of her bright smiles. "If you're not meeting someone, please join me."

David pulled out a chair and sat. "Thank you so much."

"This is wonderful," Catherine said enthusiastically. "It will give us a chance to get to know each other better."

David readied himself to eat. "Tell me about yourself."

Catherine dabbed her napkin on her lips. "There's not much to tell. I have a small apartment not far from the office, so it's very convenient. My commute is only a five-minute walk, so I don't need to worry about traffic or parking."

"How about family?"

She frowned and sadness painted her face. "I lost both my parents when they died in a car accident a few years ago. I miss them both very much. My dad always called me his princess and made me feel so loved and cared for."

David felt her pain and looked deeply into her eyes. "You were very close to your dad?"

"Yes. I looked up to him, and I guess now I measure men by his standards." A tear in the corner of her eye sparkled in the light. "That's why I don't date much. Most of the men my age can't live up to my expectations." She raised her head and smiled. "I think that's why I'm attracted to men who are older than I am. Men require extra time to transform into a fine wine."

David grinned, trying to lighten the mood. "So you think men are slower to mature than women, do you?"

Catherine shrugged her shoulders, "What can I say?"

They bantered back and forth throughout the rest of their lunch. David recognized she was very mature for her age, yet she still possessed a youthful playfulness. She had an easy way about her that he found very attractive.

He was so drawn to her that he felt a twinge of guilt. He finished his lunch just in time to head back to the office.

Catherine suggested she should speed ahead so they didn't enter the building together. "I realize how easily rumors can get started, and often it's best to be discrete. I certainly don't want to be the cause of any problems for you."

"Don't be silly," he told her. "There's nothing wrong with a boss having an occasional lunch with his secretary."

As they headed back to the office, he noticed a man who had been watching them in the restaurant. The man now walked on the other side of the street and kept glancing at them. David asked Catherine if she knew the man, but as soon as she turned to look, the man disappeared down an alley. Although she only caught a quick glimpse of him, he didn't look familiar to her.

When they entered the office, the security guard gave them a subtle look that made David think perhaps Catherine had been right; might people really think he could still attract a young woman as beautiful as Catherine? He had to admit to himself that he enjoyed the feeling.

He buried himself in work so he could avoid the guilt he felt over his infatuation with Catherine. Had he made a mistake hiring someone so young and beautiful? He reminded himself that he was a faithful husband; Deborah and he had a great marriage.

He called Deborah and suggested they go out for dinner, but she had already made plans. He suspected her plans involved another church meeting and was disappointed she wouldn't make time for him.

The anger he felt over the perceived rejection was magnified by the attention he received from Catherine.

CHAPTER SIX

THE DAY DEBORAH HAD EAGERLY AWAITED FINALLY ARRIVED: PAUL and Mary Evans were coming to dinner. Deborah was anxious for her and David to make friends who were not business or political affiliates, people who would be friends for the sole purpose of being friends. Friends whose professions differed enough from theirs that they could put shop talk on the shelf.

David agreed with Deborah's assessment they had dedicated too much of their time to their professions and consequently never taken time to cultivate any close friendships with other couples. However, he didn't share her enthusiasm for meeting this particular couple. What could he possibly have in common with a minister psychologist?

Nevertheless, as he knew this was important to Deborah, he purposed to put his best foot forward and enthusiastically welcome these potential new friends.

To his surprise, Paul was an ordinary guy. If David hadn't already known he was a minister, nothing in their conversation would have led him to that conclusion. In fact, Paul too was a car lover and currently restoring a '57 Chevrolet convertible. When David told him he had a 1998 Porsche Boxster, Paul's face lit up.

"You've got to be kidding," Paul said.

David raised his eyebrows. "No, I'm not. Do you want to take a quick ride before dinner?"

"You bet I do."

David led Paul through the kitchen and turned to Deborah and Mary with a little boy's excitement on his face. "Excuse us, ladies. We are going outside to play cars."

Deborah tilted her head at Mary. "Don't tell me Paul is a car nut, too."

"He sure is," replied Mary as her lips fell into a pout. "Sometimes I think he would rather be with his Chevy than with me."

Paul leaned forward and kissed her forehead. "Not true. You're my only real love."

The two men waved goodbye and headed out the door.

The minute Paul's gaze fell upon the Boxster, his eyes widened and his jaw dropped. David's black beauty glistening in the late day sun, its sleek lines beckoning for a driver to run it and run it hard.

"Wow!" Paul exclaimed.

"It's a 2.5-liter, six-cylinder, five-speed manual, producing 201 horsepower at six thousand RPMs, and it's fully loaded," David said without waiting for Paul to ask. "You won't believe all the features it has, considering its age." He moved around the car like he was performing a commercial. He placed his hand under the sideview mirror. "The outdoor mirrors are power adjustable and heated." Next, he pointed out the headlight cleaners and many safety features, including traction control and front and side airbags. He led Paul to the back of the car and opened the trunk. "The mid-car engine allows for a large rear trunk and a small front trunk, giving you an unusual amount of storage space for such a sporty vehicle." David continued his salesmanship, opening the passenger door and inviting Paul to sit. "As you can see, it has a beautiful leather interior, including steering wheel trim, and for your listening pleasure an incredible sound system."

David shut Paul's door, walked around the car, and sat in the driver's seat. He started the car.

"As impressive as all this is, nothing says Porsche more than driving it." David flipped the catch and pushed the button to lower the retractable roof. As they pulled away, he knew they both felt the same excitement. There was really nothing like riding a Porsche.

The rural area David lived in allowed him to put the car through some exciting paces. Once David felt they had driven far enough for Paul to experience the joy of the car, he spun it into a 180-degree turn, stopped, and told Paul to switch seats with him so he could drive back.

Paul's face exploded into a smile bigger than a child's on Christmas morning. It was a pleasure for David to watch as Paul got behind the wheel. Once they got back, Paul exited the car with the same word he had used when first looking at it: "Wow!"

In that short time, David bonded with Paul more than he had thought possible. They became quick friends. As they went back into the house, it was evident that the girls were having a similar experience, their laughter and chatter flowing from the kitchen.

"Did you boys have a good time playing outside?" Deborah asked.

"Indeed," Paul said. "We had a nice leisurely drive down a beautiful country road."

Deborah laughed. "I bet you did."

They all chitchatted throughout dinner as they sipped on wine. David was amazed with how comfortable they were with each other, although they had just met.

As Deborah poured the coffee, David decided to ask Paul the question he had been wondering about since Deborah had first told him about the minister. "Paul, I'm curious about something. Deborah told me you were a Christian minister, but you also work as a psychologist. What prompted your choice?"

Paul leaned back in his chair and folded his hands in a prayer-like position. "After becoming a minister, I went to India on a mission trip. During that time, some things happened to shake my faith and make me realize I had issues to come to grips with before I could feel competent leading a congregation.

I needed to understand God's plan for my life before I could help others connect with God's plan for their lives. I had a degree in psychology which provided me a place to park while I worked through these issues."

"I'm surprised." David slowly rotated his coffee cup. "After going through all the education required to be a minister, one might think you had already straightened all those issues out. I always thought of ministers as people who had all the answers."

Paul chuckled. "Many people believe that, but nothing could be further from the truth. As you pursue God, you find that He doesn't do things our way. He said, 'My ways are not your ways.' He is so far out of our league that it takes a lifetime for us to even begin to understand His ways."

"So you believe God has a plan for each person?"

"Yes, I do."

David smiled. "It's funny. Not too long ago, I was reading an article about the purpose of life. I've been thinking about it ever since."

"So what were your thoughts?"

David leaned back in his chair and crossed his arms, "Well, I wrestled with a lot—the mess the world is in and the misery it causes. That suggests there is no God, but on the other side of the coin, I find it hard to believe that such an intricate and complex world just exploded into being. So far my inclination lies on the side of there being a God. Now, having said that, I have no clue as to why God would have bothered creating human beings. They don't seem to be worth the effort. In fact, I suspect He would be sad with the outcome."

"Can't say I haven't wondered myself why God loves us, but He says He does," Paul said. "I once heard a story about a young couple who were madly in love. They married and had a wonderful relationship. Their love bloomed to such an extent that they felt an inner need to share it. They wanted to have a child, but they realized there was no guarantee how this child would affect their lives. They decided to take the chance. In its purest form, love begs to be shared. If God indeed is a lover, as Christians understand Him to be, it is only natural that He wants to share or expand His love. God knew about the potential for hurt and suffering love can bring, but He deemed it worth the effort. He planned to have a family. So the simple answer to why God created humans is that He wants you, me, and everyone else to be His children so He can love, teach, support, and share with us all He has."

"Wow!" David said. "That provides ample food for thought. Perhaps we can talk more about this when I meet with you to work on your Chevy?"

"Sounds good to me."

Deborah frowned at Paul "While you're on this deep subject, I too have a question for you."

"And what is it you want to know?"

"How have you managed to get David to agree to work on your Chevy after only knowing him for hours? I can't get him to do anything around here!"

"Oh come on!" David smiled. "You know if you bought a '57 Chevy, I'd help you work on it."

They all laughed and Deborah suggested they move out to the pool area to finish their coffee. The night was beautiful, the sky bursting with stars and the moon full. They even saw a shooting star dart across the sky.

What a beautiful end to a wonderful evening, thought Deborah. The dinner party was everything she had hoped it would be.

CHAPTER SEVEN

DENNIS CAIN, DISGUISED AS A MUCH OLDER MAN, WAITED FOR HIS new love interest to exit her apartment building. He had first seen her at lunch with a man he thought might be her father. Dennis had been taken by her beauty. As he'd observed her over the past few weeks, he hadn't seen her with any men, but he wanted to find out more about her before he committed to a relationship with her.

Today's objective was to find out where she worked and what her apartment number was. Dennis was anxious to try the new camera imbedded in his hat, which could be controlled from a remote in his pocket. He already had some good pictures of her, but he wanted more.

Once he knew her apartment number, he would make a plan to get in and set up cameras to give him more intimate pictures. He would also be able to get the information he needed to hack into her computer.

As Catherine left her apartment building, Dennis got some good pictures and discretely followed her to work. It was only a few blocks. He noted that she worked at Star Investments and jotted down the office hours. He planned to return and follow her home to find out her apartment number. Everything was going according to plan.

Catherine had eased into her new job and developed a routine of opening the office and having David's coffee and messages waiting for him when he arrived. They got along exceptionally well on both a business and social level. They had even gone out for lunch quite a few times.

She liked his company. In fact, she found David very attractive and suspected he felt the same about her. She could read between the lines that David wasn't totally happy with the relationship between him and his wife. Although Catherine hadn't yet met David's wife Deborah, she suspected her to be cold and demanding. A typical judge. David deserved someone who would pamper and care for him.

Each morning when David came into work, he and Catherine took some time over coffee to discuss current events. Then they went over the schedule for the day.

Catherine's weekend had been quiet. The only new thing in her life was a computer that was acting up. It appeared to be exceptionally slow and she feared it may have a virus.

David suggested he could have a look at it and maybe run some virus detection programs. Catherine told him she didn't want to impose, but he assured her it was no problem. As he had plans to meet with his new friend Paul that evening, they scheduled his visit for Wednesday after work.

Catherine had a difficult time keeping her mind on work for the remainder of the day. She remembered from previous discussions that Deborah didn't get home until late on Wednesdays, so she knew David would be available for dinner that night. Plans started formulating in her mind: clean the apartment, buy some wine, and plan a dinner menu. She wanted the meal to be planned in such a way that it looked effortless and reflected her culinary expertise.

Most importantly, she would have to delete the emails she'd sent to her friend Lisa. Catherine and Lisa played a game where they described the hot relationships they had going on in their lives.

Although they both knew the stories were fictional, they looked forward to the other's updates. Of late, Catherine's accounts had revolved around the steamy office romance she and David were experiencing. Certainly she didn't want David to accidentally come across these emails while investigating her computer problem.

At the end of the day, Catherine closed up the office and headed for the elevator. On the short walk home, her mind shuffled through the details of her Wednesday night plan.

She unlocked the lobby door to her apartment complex and held it open for an elderly gentleman behind her. Once in the elevator, she made her selection for the third floor and asked the gentleman, "What floor would you like?"

"Third floor please."

When the doors opened, Catherine proceeded to her apartment and the man continued down the hall.

———

After Catherine entered her apartment, Dennis returned to the elevator and went back down to the lobby. His mission was accomplished; he now knew Catherine lived in apartment 311. Armed with this information, he could start in earnest to acquire a key, bug her apartment, and hack into her computer.

He was so excited to get to know Catherine better. Would she be the girl of his dreams? Only time would tell.

CHAPTER EIGHT

DAVID AND PAUL HAD AGREED TO MEET FOR DINNER BEFORE working on the car. They chose a new chain restaurant that had opened near where Paul stored his Chevy.

Once they finished their dinner and had ordered dessert and coffee, David found himself curious regarding Paul's earlier statement about having his faith challenged on a mission in India. He asked Paul if he would mind telling him more about that. Paul didn't mind, but he would have to go back to before he became a Christian for the story to make sense.

"I grew up in a very rough neighborhood where being a member of a gang was almost a necessity for survival. I didn't like the things I had to do in order to get by, but I saw no alternative.

"A few kids in the neighborhood were Christians and they didn't follow the same rules everyone else did. That resulted in them being chastised for not complying. In a strange way, I respected their strength, but their holier-than-thou attitude made me and the others look bad so we bullied them at every opportunity.

"One particular boy by the name of Jackson stood out. It became an obsession for me to break him. I bullied him and beat him every time I had any occasion to."

Paul moved his dinner plate to one side and held up his coffee cup, motioning for the waitress to get him a refill. He turned back to David and continued his story.

"One evening when my gang was out creating havoc, we ran into a rival gang and a huge battle ensued. I was shot and lay on the sidewalk being kicked mercilessly in the ribs and head. The rest of my gang ran for their lives and left me there."

David frowned. "They just left you and ran?"

"They sure did."

"I can't believe they'd do such a thing. So what happened to you?"

"Who should come along but Jackson?" Paul said. "He scooped me up and physically carried me to the hospital. He arranged for my father to be contacted and waited at the hospital for him to arrive. My dad wasn't sympathetic with the mess I was in. Since I was unconscious, he saw no point to hanging around. He returned to work.

"When finally I came to, I could hear a voice praying beside me. I opened my eyes to see who it was and let out a yell that shook the whole building.

"'I can't see! I can't see!' I yelled over and over again.

Jackson ran to get a nurse, who came in and tried to settle me down. She explained that the trauma to my head had caused the loss of vision.

"'Most often the blindness is temporary,' the nurse said, 'but the doctor will need to run more tests before he can determine your situation.'"

"You must have been terrified," David said.

"Yes, I was."

The waitress arrived to refill their coffees. Paul waited until she left before continuing.

"Once the nurse left the room, I heard a voice say, 'Paul, it's Jackson from school. I'm the one who found you lying on the street in a pool of blood and brought you to the hospital. Your dad was here, but he had to go back to work. I decided to stay with you. Is there anything I can get you?'"

Paul put his elbows on the table, holding his coffee cup in his hands.

"I remembered who Jackson was, and was shocked that he would want to help me. When I asked why, he answered so nonchalantly: 'Because you needed help.'

"I replied, 'But I pushed you around and made fun of you.'

"'You certainly did, but as you know, I'm a Christian and that means I follow the teachings of Jesus. We are to forgive those who mistreat us because He has forgiven us our sins.'

"I told him, 'Based on what I've seen, I doubt you've ever sinned. That's what irritates me about you. You're too damned good.'

"'You're wrong. Sin is doing anything contrary to God's will, and we all sin, myself included. Unfortunately, the consequence of sin is that it separates us from God, and without God our future is hell.'

"'Hold on a minute. Are you saying you believe in hell?'

"'I believe in a heaven and a hell,' he said.

"I laughed at him. 'So you're saying people don't die?'

"He replied confidently. 'The body will die, but the spirit will live on eternally. Those who have accepted God's gift of Jesus will live in heaven with Him. Everyone else will be banished away from God into hell.'

"Now he was making me angry. 'Well, to me that sounds harsh and unfair. You go to heaven and I go to hell. I've got some news for you, Mr. Know-It-All. You can go to hell!' I glared at Jackson. 'Get out of my room.'

"Jackson stood and gently said, 'It's been a tough day for you, so I'll leave you to rest and come back tomorrow to see how you're doing. Is there anything I can bring you?'

"I shook my head from side to side. 'I just don't get you, Jackson. You're so different than everyone else I know.' I felt bad that I had gotten mad after all he had done for me. With much difficulty, I told him, 'I'm sorry for my outburst and I want to thank you for all you've done. Maybe tomorrow we can talk more about your God.'

"Jackson smiled and said, 'Okay, see you tomorrow.'"

"I can't believe this kid," said David. "He certainly was focused."

Paul nodded. "And it didn't end there. Unlike my father, who only visited occasionally and for very short periods of time, Jackson visited me every single day. Upon my release, my body healed nicely but I still couldn't see. The doctor had no idea if or when I might ever regain my sight. I didn't know how I would manage without my vision.

"Jackson continued to visit me at home. This nerd and I actually became friends. I confided in him that I was terrified of what lay ahead and had no idea of what to do next. He told me about a minister who was visiting his church, someone who had been used by God on many occasions to heal people. He encouraged me to go with him to church that night.

"My fear of getting around without my vision, compounded by going to church, was almost more than I could conquer. However, with Jackson's help, I attended the service.

"As this minister preached, something started to happen in me. It was like electricity flowed through my body. I thought maybe I was having a heart attack.

"Then the minister said, 'There is a young man here tonight who is having a problem with his vision, and God wants to show him that Jesus is indeed his Savior. All he need do is come to the front and accept God's help.'

"I can't explain how eager I was to go forward, but somehow I knew it was what I needed to do. Jackson helped me to the front, and when we reached the minister, he laid his hands on my head and began to pray. I don't remember what he prayed, but the energy that had been pulsating through my body increased and suddenly, like a flash of lightning, my vision was restored. I couldn't speak. All I could do was cry and cry." A tear formed in the corner of Paul's eye. "I knew at that moment that this Jesus whom Jackson had told me about was real—and if that was true, everything else Jackson told me was true. There was a God and He wanted me in His family. Wow! I was so amazed about this new truth that I wanted to find out everything I could about Jesus and His teachings. I went to every Bible study I could take in and learned so many new things. My entire life was changing.

"My old gang members felt sorry for me because they thought I had suffered a mental collapse due to the beating I took. Although I wanted to help them come to Jesus, they wanted nothing to do with me. Even my own father thought I had gone off the deep end. He pretty much disowned me as a son and left me to go on my own.

"I knew very quickly that I wanted to be a minister. I wanted God to use me to help others experience what I had experienced. The problem was that without my father's help, I didn't have the financial resources to take the necessary training." Paul used his finger to wipe a tear from his eye. "Once again, Jackson had the answer. He got a group of his friends to join us in prayer for the necessary funds for me to go to ministry school. Eventually my prayers were answered and funding became available through the church I attended. So off I went to become a minister."

"So where did the problem come in?" asked David.

"Be patient, I'm almost there," replied Paul. "As soon as I graduated, I was offered a position with the same minister who had been used to heal me. He was now doing large healing services in foreign countries. Our very first mission trip was to India. I watched with excitement the impact his preaching and healing had on the people who came to the services. My faith grew in leaps and bounds as I saw healing after healing and thousands of people accept Jesus as Savior.

"Originally my role was very much in the background. I helped to set up and tear down as we moved from place to place, and I was also part of a team that prayed while the service was in process. Eventually I was promoted to the prayer team who prayed with those who came forward to receive Jesus. As I observed all that was taking place, I was in awe of the life-changing power of God.

"My faith was rocked the day I found out that a person I had helped to come to Jesus the night before had been killed because he had become a Christian. How could this happen, I wondered? Why would Jesus let that happen? Although many people around me explained that God doesn't always act the way we anticipate, I couldn't get my mind around what had happened. I knew I had to come to grips with this before I could ever be of real value to God as a minister. So I returned home and set up my psychology practice and started searching for the answers I needed. And there you have my life story up to date."

"Wow, all this is so foreign to me," David mused. "It sounds like fantasy or science fiction. I realize you sincerely believe in these so-called miracles, but I have a problem accepting that such things happen."

"I understand completely," replied Paul. "There was a time when I felt the same. We can talk more about this later, but if we don't get to the garage we'll never get any work done on the Chevy."

CHAPTER NINE

As Deborah entered the courtroom, the bailiff said, "All rise. The court is now in session, the Honorable Judge Deborah MacDonald presiding."

Deborah sat behind the bench. "Be seated," she said, smiling as she looked around the courtroom. "Good morning, all. Let's not waste any time. Would the plaintiff's lawyer, Mr. Baker, present his opening remarks?"

Mr. Baker pushed back his chair and stood. "Thank you, Your Honor. The plaintiff will show that Ms. Cate Curte, an exotic dancer, was wrongfully terminated and that this termination was also a breach of the Human Rights Act, as it was based on age discrimination.

"After having worked for Starlight Nightclub for six years, and having not received any complaints from her employer, Mr. Grant, he called her into his office and coldly stated, 'Your time here is up.' She was given two weeks' notice and during that time was required to continue working and there would be no further settlement pertaining to this termination.

"Since a large part of Ms. Curte's remuneration is received by tips, our contention is any potential settlement regarding loss of wages due to wrongful dismissal should be based on income from employment including a sizeable amount for tips. Ms. Curte can produce income tax assessments showing the amount of tips reported as taxable income.

"Ms. Curte has now found work at another establishment and her employer will testify her start date was three months after her dismissal from Starlight Nightclub. Her current employer will also testify to her ability to capably perform her duties.

"We seek a wrongful dismissal settlement of eighteen thousand dollars. As Starlight Night Club was the first place Ms. Curte worked as an exotic dancer, she did not realize that the failure of her employer to pay vacation and holiday pay was not an industry standard.

"We will prove that the amount of payment due to her in this regard is nine thousand dollars. This represents vacation and holiday pay earned and never paid to her during the four years of her employment. Additionally, we seek twenty-five thousand dollars for pain and suffering due to the mental anguish created by the employer's age discrimination and five thousand dollars for related court costs.

"We contend this discrimination is no less destructive to a person's well-being than discrimination based on race or sex. Unfortunately, Your Honor, our society is only now starting to wake up to the terrible abuse that is taking place through age discrimination. It is only in recent years that the word ageism has been added to our dictionaries. Ageism is defined as the stereotyping of and discrimination against individuals or groups because of their age. It is a set of beliefs, attitudes, norms, and values used to justify age-based prejudice and discrimination.

"The greatest danger of discrimination of any kind is that when the lies are repeated often enough, the victims themselves start believing the stereotyping used to discriminate against them. Society has a history of marginalizing members who do not fall into its current ideal. My client believes she has a duty to stand up against such discrimination, to send a message to those who would abuse that it will not be tolerated and to let those who are currently being discriminated against know there is protection available under the law. Thank you, Your Honor."

"Thank you Mr. Baker." Deborah straightened up her pages of notes and set them aside. "Mr. Gobel, you may now present the opening remarks for the defense."

Mr. Gobel stood. "Thank you, Your Honor. The defense maintains that the decision to terminate Ms. Curte had nothing to do with age discrimination. The owner is changing the focus of his business and targeting younger customers. He believes this is necessary in order for the business to remain profitable. Every business owner should have the right to make the decisions they deem necessary in order to protect their investment and produce a reasonable return on it.

"Concerning vacation and holiday pay, the defendant contends it was understood at the time of hire that vacation and holiday pay were factors considered in the weekly salary and as such were included in her weekly amount. This is evidenced in that, prior to her dismissal, Ms. Curte never brought this up with her employer. Thank you, Your Honor."

———

As Dennis Cain listened to the opening remarks from the gallery, he photographed Judge MacDonald through a new mini camera he had previously used with much success. He had to get to know her so he could effectively punish her husband for fooling around with his new love, Catherine. He knew from the emails Catherine had sent to her friend Lisa that something was going on between her and her boss. It annoyed Dennis that David MacDonald, an older man, had the nerve to get in the way of his relationship with Catherine. Dennis planned on teaching David a lesson he would not soon forget. After all, David was not only fooling with Dennis' girl; he was being unfaithful to this lovely woman who sat before him presiding over the case. What would be her verdict when she found out David was running around on her?

Dennis found the plaintiff, Ms. Curte, to be a very attractive lady and he snapped a few pictures of her. She was certainly not the type of women he would consider girlfriend material, but she could be a fun one-night stand. Perhaps he should check her out at her new workplace, or maybe even visit her some evening at her home.

Deborah thanked Mr. Gobel for his opening and suggested this would be a good time to adjourn for lunch.

Back in her office, she asked the bailiff, "Charles, did you notice the elderly gentleman in the gallery?"

"I did not," he replied. "Why are you asking?"

"I don't know. It's just that he has deep penetrating eyes that left me feeling unsettled. Pay no mind to me. Go and enjoy your lunch."

Judge MacDonald ran some errands over lunch and chose to save time by grabbing a bite from a drive-thru. Unbeknownst to her, every place she went Dennis was right behind, picking up all the information he could about her. He was very proud about how good of a detective he was. He knew all the tricks of the trade and within weeks he could know anyone better than their best friends. Today had provided him with much information about Mrs. MacDonald, and this evening he would check out Ms. Curte. Dennis grew excited about what the future held.

As the afternoon session began, Mr. Baker called a gerontologist to the stand. "Dr. Preston, could you please tell the court, how old is old?"

"As aging is a process and not a point in time, your question is impossible to answer," Dr. Preston said. "Old is a comparative word used to position a person's location along the continuum of life.

Where you position the crossover between young and old will vary depending on many factors, and those factors will change from person to person. One might say if you are more than halfway to the average number of years for life expectancy, you're old. Another may feel a person is not old until they are three-quarters of the way. Life expectancy is only one factor that may be considered in aging. There are other factors, such as physiological changes that typically lead to functional decline and increased susceptibility to certain diseases. In general, all living things deteriorate over time."

"Thank you, Dr. Preston." Mr. Baker started to turn away but then stopped and turned back. "One more question for you. Does that mean younger is better?"

"No, definitely not. Age itself should never be used as the determining factor of a person's abilities. No two people age the same and therefore you cannot apply one set of rules to them. I have a patient who is in his eighties and can still run a full marathon. I'm sure there are many people much younger, myself included, who are not currently able to do so."

"Thank you, Dr. Preston. I have no further questions." Mr. Baker returned to his seat.

"Do you have any questions for the witness, Mr. Gobel?" Deborah asked.

"Yes, Your Honor, I do." Mr. Gobel stood and approached the stand. "Thank you, Dr. Preston, for your informative testimony. I ask you to look at Ms. Curte and tell me if you find her attractive."

"Yes, I do."

"Would you suspect there might be people in this courtroom who disagree with you?"

"There may be."

"How likely would it be that someone who disagreed with you would be younger than you?"

"I have no real way of knowing."

"Would you expect, on average, that the wider the age span between two people, the less likely they would be physically attracted to one another?"

"That question would be outside my area of expertise."

"How about you, Doctor? Would you be attracted to a woman twice your age?"

Mr. Baker stood up and shouted, "Objection, Your Honor! Mr. Gobel is leading the witness and soliciting opinions outside the area of his expertise."

"You don't have to answer the question," Deborah told the witness.

"Thank you, Dr. Preston," Mr. Gobel said. "That's all the questions I have for you."

"You may step down," said Deborah. "Do you have another witness to call to the stand, Mr. Baker?"

"Yes, Your Honor. I call to the stand Mr. Drummond." The court waited as the man stepped forward and took his place behind the stand to testify. "Mr. Drummond, would you tell the court your profession?"

"I am a chartered accountant and I specialize in tax return preparation for professional entertainers."

"Is Ms. Curte one of your clients?" Mr. Baker asked.

"Yes, she is."

"Do you have other clients employed as exotic dancers?"

"Yes, I do."

"Would their numbers and variety of workplaces be sufficient that you would have a sense of an exotic dancer's average income?"

"Yes, within the boundaries of our city. I have no knowledge of those working in other areas."

"What would be the average pay per year?"

"I would estimate it to be approximately twenty-five thousand to thirty thousand per year, plus tips."

"Are tips normally reported when you prepare a tax return?"

"Yes, they are."

"Are these amounts significant?"

"They can be anywhere from ten percent to more than the amount of the salary."

"Without asking you to divulge any privileged information, would you tell us how Ms. Curtes' tips compare to your other clients?"

"Her tips are among the highest of any of my clients."

"Thank you Mr. Drummond. I have no further questions."

Deborah turned to Mr. Gobel. "Mr. Gobel, do you have any questions for Mr. Drummond?"

"Yes, Your Honor, I do. Mr. Drummond, how are tips accounted for?"

"They are the responsibility of the individual to track."

"Are all people so honest that they would report all their tips?"

"I have no way of knowing how accurate these figures are."

"Would it be fair to say the accuracy between tips reported from one client to another may be distorted by the varying degree of each individual's honesty?"

"I'm not in a position to know."

"Thank you, Mr. Drummond. I have no further questions."

"You may step down," said Deborah. "We will adjourn for the day. Court will resume at ten o'clock tomorrow morning."

CHAPTER TEN

CATHERINE CHECKED OUT HER APARTMENT BEFORE LEAVING FOR work. Tonight was the night David had agreed to come over to work on her computer. She had one last look around her apartment before leaving and gave herself a thumb up. It looked great and she was ready to receive her guest.

She went to work full of anticipation. Catherine arrived before David, prepared his messages, made coffee, and arranged everything on his desk just as he would have laid it out.

As was their custom, before starting work they socialized for five or ten minutes while enjoying coffee. Catherine confirmed that David hadn't forgotten their evening plans. She told him not to stop to eat, as she had prepared a meal for them.

David's face showed surprise. "You didn't need to do all that."

"I will enjoy the opportunity to pamper you," she replied in a flirtatious voice. "After all, you are going to work on my computer."

David felt a wave of excitement about this new development. That feeling was followed immediately by guilt.

Catherine turned to leave the office and said over her shoulder, "Don't forget you have a new client who will be here any moment."

She no sooner got to her desk when the door opened and in walked a distinguished and fit looking man who appeared to be in his mid-forties. He had a boyish face and very friendly smile. He took two steps into the office and stopped dead, obviously taken by surprise.

"This is not the usual financial office look," he exclaimed.

"It is different," replied Catherine. "I hope you like it."

"Indeed I do."

"I feel transported to a wonderful tropical island," the visitor said, referring to the recent renovations.

Catherine stood and reached out her hand to him. "You must be Mr. Cain."

"I am indeed, but please call me Dennis." He took her hand in his firm grip. He drank in the beauty of her magnetic blue eyes and welcoming smile. Her beautiful navy blue dress hugged her body and accentuated her figure. It had a high neckline. She was elegant, sexy, and business-like all in one. Dennis lost himself in his appreciation of her beauty and realized he had extended his handshake beyond what was customary.

Catherine's voice interrupted his thoughts. "Could I get you coffee or tea?"

He released her hand as his cheek reddened. "A black coffee would be wonderful."

"Have a seat and I will tell Mr. MacDonald you're here."

Within a minute, David came out to greet Mr. Cain. "Pleased to meet you, Mr. Cain. My name is David MacDonald. Come with me to my office and Catherine will bring your coffee in to you."

Over coffee, the two men got to know each other and agreed to use first names only. Even though Dennis suspected David was having a relationship with Catherine, the girl of his dreams, he somehow couldn't help but like David.

Dennis perused the unusual artwork on the walls, then came to rest on a large-screen TV directly opposite him. David could see the question on Dennis' face and told him that the screen was connected to his computer so the files referenced during meetings could easily be displayed. Dennis was impressed by the attention to detail evident.

As the meeting progressed, David was pleasantly surprised by the amount of money Dennis wished to invest. He would indeed be a welcome addition to his client base. Dennis gave no indication of where his money came from, but he worked for the Canadian Security Intelligence Service (CSIS). David put aside any worries he may have had regarding the source of the money. He agreed to prepare an investment plan for Dennis to review at a future meeting.

On the way out, Dennis stopped to thank Catherine for the coffee. This gave him a chance to once again enjoy her beauty and bathe himself in the aroma of her exquisite perfume. He had already identified the scent as Gucci Guilty; he had seen it on the vanity when he had been to her apartment. As he left the office, he was pleased with the success of his visit.

———

After lunch, David received a call from Deborah advising him that her normal Wednesday work meeting had been cancelled. She wondered if he would be free to join her for dinner out.

David felt tension rise in him like that of a child caught with his hand in the cookie jar. He couldn't bring himself to tell Deborah the truth, for he expected it would be misunderstood. He lied and told her he had arranged to meet with a client, knowing she wouldn't be home.

Deborah was disappointed, as they had spent so little time together lately. But she understood. She hung up the phone, saying, "See you when you get home. Love you."

David's earlier guilt resurrected, and once again he had to convince himself that he really had nothing to feel guilty about. All he was doing was helping a friend.

At the end of the day, David and Catherine locked up the office and Catherine rode home in David's car. This was her first time in his Porsche and she loved the luxurious feel of it.

Catherine told David she had arranged for him to park in front of the superintendent's garage, since there wasn't adequate visitors parking. The superintendent, Mrs. Field, was coming out of the garage upon their arrival so Catherine introduced them.

Inside the apartment, David went directly to the computer on a rolltop desk and Catherine asked if he needed anything.

"No," David replied. "I'll start by downloading an anti-virus program and run it to see if anything shows up."

"If you need anything, just shout. I'm going to change into more comfortable clothes and start dinner."

While David was waiting for the download to finish, he looked around at the pleasant but small apartment. It reminded him of one of the first apartments he and Deborah had shared. Although they'd had so much less back then, in so many ways they had been happier.

While lost in thought, Catherine returned with a glass of wine for him. She was now in a tight pair of blue jeans and a sporty tank-top that revealed her flat stomach. It was all David could do to keep his eyes from traveling to her stomach. He thanked her for the wine and kept his eyes on her as she turned and strolled in her bare feet back to the kitchen.

The application of the anti-virus program failed to reveal any problems, so David ran another program designed to detect and re-solve problems relating to slow computer performance. As the prob-lem only occurred periodically and the computer had ample pro-cessing capability, only time would tell how effective his efforts were.

The meal Catherine prepared was spectacular. Drawing from her French heritage, she served a fresh salad made with raw spin-ach, caramelized shallots, toasted walnuts, dried cranberries, and a bit of goat cheese. This complemented a wonderful tourtiere. David found this French meat pie to be absolutely delicious. They enjoyed the meal with a wonderful red wine and easy-flowing conversa-tion. The dessert was maple pudding chomeur, a wickedly sweet cake-pudding served with ice cream.

David couldn't remember ever having a better meal. He told Catherine her food compared favorably to the finest restaurants he had been in.

Catherine suggested he relax on the sofa while she got coffee. Upon returning, she sat beside him. Her arm and leg occasionally brushed against him as the conversation continued. He found himself becoming aroused and knew he would have to leave quickly or he may do something he would later regret. He thanked Catherine for a lovely meal and told her the time was late and he needed to be going.

She thanked him for the work he had done and told him how much she had enjoyed having him for dinner.

As he started his car and pulled away, he saw Mrs. Field peeking through the blinds.

He headed home feeling guilty about the marvelous time he had with Catherine.

———

Dennis Cain was furious about what he had witnessed. It wasn't bad enough that Catherine was spending time with another man, but why would she choose a man old enough to be her father? He made a promise that he would make David pay for fooling around with his girl.

CHAPTER ELEVEN

Diary Entry, May 15, 2013

Thought of the day: "When they call the roll in the Senate, the Senators do not know whether to answer 'Present' or 'Not guilty.'" (Theodore Roosevelt)

I had trouble sleeping last night because I felt guilty about having had dinner with Catherine at her apartment and maybe enjoying it a little too much. I did not actually do anything wrong, but for some reason I feel guilty.

I'm going to meet with Paul tonight to help him work on his car. He should be able to help me. The problem is I don't know how safe it is to tell him about what occurred. Even though I didn't do anything wrong, I'm not comfortable telling Deborah anything about having dinner with Catherine—and now I'm wondering about how much to tell Paul. Why is this, if I did nothing wrong?

This seems to be the way my life is going. I don't remember being so unsure about the little details when I was younger. Now that life should be so much easier, it seems to be getting more complicated than ever.

It's time for me to leave for work and I feel somewhat uncomfortable about how to approach morning coffee with

Catherine. I'm not at all sure what she is expecting me to say about our meal and time together last night.

————

DAVID HEADED DOWN TO GRAB BREAKFAST; DEBORAH HAD ALREADY left for work. He tossed some bread into the toaster and prepared a bowl of cereal. The day was as dreary as his somber attitude. It never ceased to amaze him how strong an effect the sun had on one's attitude. He began reading the morning paper but decided he didn't need to be further demoralized by what was going on in the world.

He headed out the door munching on the remainder of his toast, somewhat lifted by the sight of his gorgeous Porsche.

When he arrived at the office, Catherine already had his mail sorted and a coffee sitting on his desk in the usual spot. They had their customary morning chat. She started the conversation by thanking him for the work he had done on her computer. He in turn thanked her for the lovely meal and told her what a lovely apartment she had. The conversation felt so artificial to him; it was like they were following a script, each of them saying what was expected of them. He hesitated to tell her how much he had enjoyed the evening as he didn't want her to get the wrong idea.

He struggled to determine what last night had really been all about. On the one hand, Catherine seemed to be letting him know she was attracted to him; on the other hand, his common sense told him this was probably the furthest thing from her mind. Perhaps his guilt was causing him to blow this way out of proportion. They'd only had dinner, after all.

What on earth is wrong with me? he wondered.

They finished their chat, went over the schedule for the day, and then Catherine left to perform her daily duties.

David called the clients who had left messages and prepared for the day's upcoming meetings. His afternoon workload would be low, so he called Deborah to see if she could join him for lunch.

Unfortunately, her schedule was such that lunch wouldn't be possible.

His day dragged on without anything too interesting happening, and he was relieved when it was finally time to leave. He'd arranged to meet Paul for an early dinner, then go to work on the Chevy.

Paul chose the restaurant; it was one David had never been to. It was called The Quiet Corner. Its claim to fame was that it had no background music, no televisions, and each table had a lockbox for cell phones and other electronic gadgets. It was a place where you could sit and talk without the many distractions that had become so common. The establishment suggested that guests set their own penalty for anyone in their group who needed to unlock the lockbox to get their electronic fix. It was a fun way to suggest that people get back to relational meals.

The restaurant itself was designed to provide a quiet environment. The booths were high to absorb sound, and clear Plexiglas divided the large space into smaller sections to provide quiet while maintaining a sense of privacy. The earthy tones of the décor and strategically placed plants encouraged one to relax.

Paul was already seated when David arrived, and he stood and waved to get David's attention. They ordered drinks and talked about the work to be done on the Chevy. As the conversation dried up and the waiter brought appetizers, David decided to talk about his adventure with Catherine and the resulting sense of guilt.

"Paul, do you mind if I ask you a question about a sense of guilt I've been experiencing? I realize you've worked all day, and I completely understand if you would prefer not to talk shop."

"Fire away. I'm all ears."

David explained what had taken place with Catherine. He expected the minister part of Paul to condemn him, but that never happened. Paul listened intently and never gave any sign of being judgmental.

"What you've described is very common," Paul said once David had finished. "I explain to my clients that guilt, initially, is an early warning system. When you're contemplating an action contrary to the inner values you have established, guilt kicks in and sets off an alarm.

"I teach my clients that this is the appropriate time to ask yourself two questions. The first being, if I take the action I'm contemplating, will I be okay with this action being known to my loved ones, peers, and the general public? The second question is this: will my intended action live up to the golden rule?

"No matter whether you make a good decision or a bad decision, the guilt alarm has a mind of its own. If it perceives that you didn't avoid the danger, it will continue to sound. Resetting this alarm can be a very difficult task. The process will require the problem to be brought out into the open and the roots uncovered. Often you need to develop new ways to deal with these root causes.

"In your situation, David, I suspect you already know the answer. You may simply need to verbalize what your guilt is telling you. Why don't you give it a try?"

Paul's advice hit David right between the eyes.

"Wow," Paul said. "Those are good questions. I certainly couldn't comply with the first. I didn't feel comfortable about telling my wife, and I wasn't even sure about telling you. So far as the golden rule, I wouldn't want Deborah to meet someone under the same circumstances.

"On the positive side, my initial guilt served me well as it urged me to quickly leave Catherine's apartment. Leaving that situation when I did may have saved me from doing something I would have regretted. I'm not ready, nor do I feel it would be beneficial, to tell Deborah about this, so I guess I need to think about the root problem and see if I can deal with it.

"It's funny, but the first thought that came to mind as you spoke was the adage that says if you play with fire, you're going to get burnt. I'm only now realizing how attracted I am to Catherine. I guess I'm at an age when men feel they need to prove themselves, and the drifting that's happening with Deborah is adding fuel to the fire.

"The problem won't be easy to deal with. It hardly seems fair to fire a perfectly good employee because I'm having problems dealing with my lust—and it probably isn't legal. On the other hand, I'm not so sure I can turn it off."

"No," said Paul. "The bigger problem is why you have this lust. That's the area I would suggest you explore."

David smiled. "Thanks for your help, Paul. I can see that I need to talk to Deborah about our relationship. It seems to me it has been slipping away and I don't know how to stop it."

"Speaking with Deborah would be an excellent place to start," Paul agreed. "I'll let you chew on that until our next deep discussion. For now, let's get out of here and get some work done on the Chevy."

When David arrived home, Deborah was curled up on her favorite chair reading. Although he was tired from the full day he'd had, he felt compelled to draw Deborah into a conversation about their relationship. He began by asking her what she was reading.

"The book is about aging," she said. "The age discrimination case I'm hearing has made me realize how ill prepared I am for the next stage of my life."

He sat in the chair opposite her. "That's amazing. I've been struggling with this very same issue. In fact, I talked with Paul about it tonight. He suggested we would benefit from getting away. We need some time together to talk about how things are changing as we age. Perhaps this would be a good time for us to consider a vacation. Get away from everything and have time to be together and talk."

"That sounds wonderful. We've had so little time together lately. Let's plan to do it."

"Okay," replied David. "Let's review our schedules tomorrow and pick a date."

David already felt closer to Deborah than he had for a long time. This was certainly a good start.

"So tell me, Deborah, what does your book say about aging?"

"The author writes about how we are heavily influenced, even manipulated, by those who want to control our behavior for their own benefit. This often results in our acceptance of ideas that are not in our best interest. Here's a particularly interesting quote: 'Who you are is often more a reflection of perception than of truth.' This is later tied to how each of our choices will have consequences. Good choices usually result in good consequences, but wrong choices tend to lead to unpleasant results. The problem is that the consequences of our choices vary in the length of time it takes before they surface. The longer the gap between choice and consequence, the more difficult it will be to correct the problem. Sometimes the appearance of consequences may take so long that once we realize what we've done, it's too late to fix it.

"Aging results from the passing of time, so many of the erroneous decisions we've made along the way come to light. An obvious example is one that comes from your area of expertise. If you spent everything you earned to maximize your enjoyment when you're young, you may be in financial trouble later. A proverb says, 'The wisdom of the wise is to give thought to their ways. They think about where they're going. But the folly of fools is deception. They keep lying to themselves.'[1]

"So I guess our desire to think about where we're going suggests we are wise people, and wise people need their sleep—so let's head off to bed."

---

1   Mark Buchanan, *The Rest of God: Restoring Your Soul by Restoring Sabbath* (Nashville, TN: Thomas Nelson, 2006), 40.

CHAPTER TWELVE

As Dennis watched Catherine sleep, he pondered the rage he felt about Catherine and David's dinner together. Although he observed no infidelity on this occasion, he knew from the emails Catherine had sent to Lisa that she had been unfaithful to him and that David had been unfaithful to his wife on several occasions. The question was, what should be their punishment? Certainly Catherine could no longer be considered for a long-term relationship; it was time to cut her out of his life. As for David, he was the one who had wrecked Dennis' relationship with Catherine and he would be made to pay dearly.

An eye for an eye sounded like fair punishment to Dennis.

Fortunately for you, David, I'm a just man, he thought, laughing. *So I'll see to it you come before a competent judge. Someone we both respect. When I'm done with you, you'll know how it feels to suffer the pain of rejection. It may take a while, but I'll make sure you get what's coming to you. That's a promise, David. That's a promise!*

Dennis threw a kiss to Catherine before he turned off his monitor and readied himself to leave for work.

The sky was a beautiful azure with not a cloud to be seen, but Dennis found no enjoyment in it. Instead he wallowed in his feelings of emptiness. Why had he been condemned to never know the love of a mother? Why did women always betray him?

He lamented that his deep craving for a meaningful relationship would never be satisfied.

As he pulled up to the security gate of the CSIS offices, the security officer greeted him by name. "Good morning, Mr. Cain. How are you today?"

"I'm fine, Tony. How is your boy Luciano making out with soccer?"

Tony beamed with pride. "He's doing extremely well, sir. Scored a goal in each of the last three games, and yesterday's goal was a last-minute winner."

"That's wonderful, Tony. I'll have to go with you to one of his games."

"That would be great, sir. I'll get you a copy of his schedule."

"Thanks. I look forward to receiving it. You have yourself a great day."

"Thank you, sir. Same to you."

Dennis parked in his personal space and headed up to his office. He was proud of who he was and what he did for a living. He doubted any of the caregivers who had been in charge of his upbringing would ever have thought he would rise in the ranks of CSIS. Dennis was a good fit here. A major requirement of working for CSIS was the ability to work on one's own and keep to oneself. This suited Dennis to a tee.

As a data exploitation analyst, he knew how important his role was in keeping Canada safe. His job was to intercept communications to discover sensitive information that might threaten national security, a job he enjoyed for the sheer challenge of it. He recognized that people would never know what he did for them; in fact, they may well be horrified to know how much Big Brother watched over them. Although he'd never had a family, he was indeed a big brother to all his fellow Canadians. They needed him. Quite frankly, they weren't terribly bright.

Case in point, this David MacDonald guy, Dennis thought. *He has a loving wife, a good life, yet he's willing to give it all up for the lust of a young woman.*

One would think a man who could build such a successful business would have more sense than that. The same greed that motivated people to accomplish great things could also lead them to destruction.

But I digress. Enough about David MacDonald. It's time to prepare some pictures I'm sure Mrs. MacDonald will find very interesting.

Dennis' Photoshop abilities allowed him to create photo manipulations that even the most skilled evaluators wouldn't be able to detect. He roared with laughter as he contemplated that these pictures would likely be sent to him to be authenticated.

As he copied and pasted images of Catherine and David into suggestive positions, he realized that he needed more information about David and his relationship with Deborah to successfully convince Deborah the pictures were authentic. He decided to take the time to set up surveillance in the MacDonald household. Not only would this provide the information he needed, it would also allow him to witness the happenings when his artwork was unveiled.

He diverted his attention to setting up a bank account in Catherine's name to which deposits from David's business account could be made. This would provide evidence that Catherine was being paid off for her silence. The fact that David's business account was managed by an accounting service that processed all his invoices and payroll made this part of the plan very easy to carry out.

He looked at his watch and realized that he needed to be on his way to a Big Brothers Big Sisters of Canada lunch meeting. He was a board member, and also a big brother himself. After all he had been through in life, he realized how important it was for a child to have someone to help them through the difficult years of growing up. The time and energy he devoted to Big Brothers Big Sisters added to the wellness of society and the country. It made him feel good to be able to contribute in such a significant way.

His current little brother, Jake, was ten years old and a joy to be with. He was a good athlete and a good student. It made Dennis proud to realize how much he had contributed to Jake's upbringing. Jake wouldn't have to grow up without knowing love or a father figure. Jake also had a good mother who loved him very much.

He enjoyed a light lunch with the other board members before the meeting started. The reports given were uplifting. To his surprise, the president of the board presented him with an award for his dedication and length of service. Dennis had difficulty successfully hiding the incredible joy he felt from receiving this award. It meant the world to him.

Dennis stayed behind to meet with a fellow board member with whom he was planning a fly-in fishing trip for the big and little brothers. This event would be unforgettable for city kids. How he wished he could have enjoyed such things when he was a kid. He looked forward to sharing the experience with Jake.

He headed back to his office feeling better about himself than he had in a long time.

CHAPTER THIRTEEN

Diary Entry, May 25, 2013

Thought of the day: "You don't develop courage by being happy in your relationships every day. You develop it by surviving difficult times and challenging adversity." (Epicurus)

When I told Paul that Deborah and I were going to follow his advice and plan a getaway, he handed me a brochure for a marriage seminar in St. Augustine, Florida. He suggested this might provide an ideal forum for Deborah and me to work on our relationship.

Although I hadn't been thinking about going to a marriage seminar, the idea does have merit and the venue is perfect. Deborah and I have always wanted to explore the sights of St. Augustine. However, I'm still not comfortable with the fact it's a Christian seminar. In spite of this, I have an inner sense that this is right for us. Needless to say, Deborah is all for it.

So, today's the day. I'm anxious to explore St. Augustine. It's the oldest continuously inhabited city in the United States. I'm looking forward to soaking up the history and architecture.

It's time to start packing so I'll be ready when the limo service arrives. We fly out of Pearson and will be picked up in Jacksonville by the resort's shuttle service.

ALTHOUGH THE TRIP TO THE AIRPORT WAS EXTREMELY BUSY, David and Deborah arrived with plenty of time to make their way through the various stages of boarding the plane. It was a beautiful day and their plane was ready for takeoff right on schedule.

As David looked out the window, he reflected on how orderly the world looked from this height. There was no evidence of the chaos—no horns beeping, no people yelling, no sirens blaring.

David loved the feeling of being suspended in midair, hanging like an ornament on a Christmas tree. Many people felt stressed when flying, but for him it was a time of peace.

He turned to Deborah and watched her read. He wondered how he could have ever thought they were no longer good for each other. At this moment, he knew they were meant to be. This vacation was exactly what they needed to recapture the loving relationship that seemed to have been slipping away.

The airplane wasn't only carrying them to their destination; it was symbolic of them being lifted to a new level in their relationship.

While observing Deborah, he tried to imagine what he would guess she did for a living if he hadn't met her before. Her long, thin neck gave her a regal look. Her dark hair fell down to her shoulders with a hint of natural curl. She was the classic beauty often referred to as the girl next door. As he continued his guessing game, one thing he knew for sure: he would never have guessed she was a judge. Perhaps a doctor; her dark captivating eyes exhibited compassion and strong confidence. The more he looked at her, the more he realized how much he loved her and what a lucky man he was to have her for a wife.

A story he had once heard popped into his mind. A man was applying for a high level sales position when he pulled out a picture of his wife and handed it to the interviewer. The man proclaimed that this was the best validation of his sales ability.

"I convinced this woman to marry me," he said.

The man was hired on the spot.

David understood how the man in the story must have felt. Deborah was much more than he deserved. He regretted his recent behavior with Catherine.

"Why are you looking at me with that strange look on your face?" Deborah asked, turning to him.

He laughed. "I was thinking about how long it's been since we've been alone together in a hotel room."

"Down, boy," she teased. "This is a Christian conference we're attending."

"So what do Christians do when they're alone in a room with a beautiful woman who just happens to be their wife?"

She grinned. "Maybe that's what they'll teach us at the marriage seminar."

"I certainly hope so."

Just then, the attendant arrived with a snack and a drink. He and Deborah clicked their plastic wine glasses together as he proposed a toast to a fantastic vacation.

———

In no time, they arrived in Jacksonville.

"Isn't it amazing how time flies when you're in an airplane?" David asked. She rolled her eyes as he giggled to himself.

They disembarked and were fortunate enough to meet up with their luggage. They had no trouble finding the shuttle. On the way, the driver told them that the resort sat on fifteen acres of land on the outskirts of St. Augustine and provided free shuttle service into the city's tourist district.

When they reached the resort, the driveway meandered through a well-treed lot until it came to a clearing. Their eyes were drawn to an amazing log cabin that blended perfectly with its surroundings, creating an overall picture of serenity, inviting one to leave the busy world behind. A long, rambling veranda and gable roof fronted the building.

The lobby was absolutely stunning, featuring a gorgeous hardwood floor and cathedral ceiling. Large windows invited sunshine into the room, providing a warm welcome.

David and Deborah checked in and the porter led the way to their room. As they walked in, they were delighted with the way the décor combined simplicity, elegance, and functionality. They stood at the door in awe.

David turned to Deborah. "These Christians sure do know how to book a conference venue!"

"They may know more than you've given them credit for."

"I'm starting to believe so."

They had hours before the registration and welcome dinner, so Deborah decided to soak in the tub and relax. David was eager to investigate the grounds. He browsed the welcoming information on the desk in their room and found a map showing walking trails on the property. He chose one of the smaller trails which he suspected would only take him twenty minutes to walk.

Not long into his walk, a marker directed his gaze to a southern live oak. The pamphlet indicated that many of these trees were more than five hundred years old, and one was even believed to be fourteen hundred years old. Spanish moss draped the tree, giving it an eerie look.

He enjoyed the light breeze as he walked and was introduced to many plants that were foreign to him. The more he walked, the more relaxed he became.

When David got back up to the room, he was glad it was almost time to head to dinner. He had worked up quite an appetite.

As they left their room, he was somewhat apprehensive about gathering with this group of Christians. He wasn't sure what to expect.

The room being used for the welcome dinner was as spectacular as everything else. Large windows overlooked a wonderful view and the log walls provided a homey feel. This same ambiance permeated the entire lodge.

The dinner setting wasn't banquet style, as he had expected, but rather intimate tables of four. Each couple was to find their nametags at the table. It was an effective setup to promote intermingling. When David and Deborah found their table, the other couple assigned to sit with them was already seated.

The man stood and reached out his hand to greet David. "Good evening. I'm Al Freeman and this is my wife Dolores."

David in turn introduced himself and Deborah.

Al was the talkative type and as soon as they all got seated he told them they were from Blandon, Pennsylvania, a suburb of Reading. David suspected they were a little younger than he and Deborah.

Al explained that he and Dolores had recently became empty nesters. With the children gone and their life goals accomplished, they suddenly realized life had flown by so quickly that they were left wondering what had happened. In their busyness, they hadn't spent enough time nurturing their relationship and needed to get to know each other in a whole new way.

"So I'm hoping this conference will help us add true intimacy to our marriage and give us direction for the future," Al finished.

As the evening went on, they had a good time getting to know their new friends. David found once again that his concerns about Christians—that they were somehow different and wouldn't make compatible friends—were totally unfounded. He now felt eager to get started with the first session, which was to be held following dinner.

The dinner offered so many choices that David and Deborah decided to each make a different choice so they could share and increase their sampling of the menu. They got to try gator tail, pilaw, and margarita flatbread before they even started on their main course. Everything was fresh and delicious.

Tea and coffee were to be served in the conference room, so off they went to the first session.

The speaker, Mr. Lloyd Matthews, had wild hair that seemed to go in every direction and big glasses that completed his nerd look.

"Each of you here tonight is different from the other and as a couple you are dealing with different challenges," Matthews said, welcoming them. "But no matter where you're at, this is the good news of the Bible: God so loved the world that Jesus came that we may have life and have it abundantly. Jesus is revered by all the major religions of the world for being a great teacher. His teachings have been tried and proven. So I can confidently assure you that if you apply His teachings, your marriage will thrive."

He went on to explain that marriage had been created by God to be a training ground for learning how to love. Unfortunately, most people don't know what love is. He challenged those in the room to define love. The atmosphere in the room filled with tension, everyone freezing in place so the instructor won't notice them and turn to them for an answer.

Matthews moved away from the center of the room so no one's vision of the screen was impaired. "The word love is misused so often in our society that it's easy to have the wrong idea of what love is. For our purpose in this seminar, we need to clarify the definition so we're all on the same page."

He clicked the remote he was holding in his hand and a definition appeared on the screen. "Love is choosing to want the betterment of another to such an extent that you are willing to give up of yourself in charity for that purpose. This is the only material we will cover this evening. For the next fifteen minutes, I want you to sit in silence, no talking to anyone else, and spend the time contemplating this application of love and what it may require of you. Write your thoughts on the paper provided."

Once the time was up, they were told to take time with their spouse that evening, in the privacy of their room, to discuss the results of their contemplation. Then they were dismissed. They were to meet up again in the same room for breakfast at nine.

Deborah and David returned to their room, exchanging few words as they rode the elevator. The session, although short, had been very impactful and they were both processing what they had heard.

Once they reached their room, David opened the bottle of wine he had purchased at the bar and poured a glass for each of them. They sat facing the large window admiring the star-filled sky. The ambience of this place surely encouraged intimate discussion.

"The word 'choosing' in the definition of love disturbs me," Deborah began. "It seems to me that you don't choose to love someone. You fall in love with them."

"I wonder if the careless way words are used contribute to the confusion we have about how to define the word love," David replied. "When someone says it was love at first sight, is that the correct word or would a word like infatuation be more accurate?"

Deborah giggled. "It would sound rather strange to hear someone say it was infatuation at first sight."

"I agree. There can be a wow factor when you meet someone, but is the romantic feeling you're talking about love?"

"Maybe not," replied Deborah. "But the idea of love being a choice seems to remove any idea of romance."

"But this definition describes what most people are looking for: to be loved as they are, fully accepted even though their flaws are known, no need to hide anything. I admit that's what I want, but I don't believe I'm personally up to the challenge of loving that way. It would require complete selflessness."

Deborah agreed that it set a high standard. "For me, this evening has raised many questions. I hope they'll be answered."

They were both tired and agreed to stop their discussion and prepare for bed.

CHAPTER FOURTEEN

Diary Entry, May 26, 2013

Thought of the day: "For this reason a man will leave his father and mother and be united to his wife, and they will become one flesh." (Genesis 2:24)

My quote today is one of the Bible verses we were given to read at yesterday's session. I'm hoping the instructors will explain the last part of it: "They will become one flesh." It's an intriguing statement.

I'm overjoyed with how well everything has been going. The flight was wonderful, our shuttle driver was excellent, the facilities are remarkable, dinner was delicious, Al and Dolores were delightful, and the opening session was thought-provoking. All in all, I would rate it an excellent day.

Although I'm looking forward to today, I suspect it's going to be demanding. Yesterday's session made me realize how much I expect and receive from Deborah, and how little I give. I don't like to face up to how selfish I am. Everything in my life is about me. I expect the world should revolve around my needs. I really do want to love Deborah the way she deserves to be loved, but I question if I can overcome my selfishness enough to place her first.

Well, Deborah has come out of the shower so it's time for me to get ready.

THE PLAN FOR THE DAY WAS TO HAVE AN EARLY BREAKFAST WITH THE group and begin the session immediately after. Breakfast was buffet-style but in keeping with the other meals—lots of choice, excellent presentation, and tasty food.

When they entered the presentation area, a huge sign read: "Don't even think about how today's subject material applies to your spouse or anyone else; focus on how it applies to you."

The topic of love was explored more fully. The instructors taught that love and relationship are distinct from each other. Although people maintain many different kinds of relationships in their lives, there is only one kind of love. The depth of relationship is determined by the level of intimacy experienced.

Three types of intimacy were discussed. The first was based on common experiences, the second was spiritual in nature, and the third sexual.

The first type of relationship was characterized by what David and Deborah had discussed with the Freemans the previous night. Many marriages were built on this type of intimacy—the partnership starting with infatuation, planning a wedding, finding a place to live, building a family, maintaining a career, and raising children. Once the children left home, empty-nesters often found they had spent little time getting to know each other. This could happen when the couple, in their busyness, never truly shared in the second, deeper spiritual intimacy.

The second type of relationship was about soulmates—when a person's partner truly knows them and accepts them despite their faults. People who had this type of relationship were much more able to have positive feelings about the empty nest. They were also more likely to be optimistic about the possibilities facing them in the new phase of their lives.

The third kind of intimacy, sexual, was the least understood. The Bible stated that something more than pleasure occurs when people have sexual intercourse, hence the Bible verse that says "The two become one flesh,"

"Visualize taking two separate pieces of paper and dabbing them here and there with glue, then sticking them together," Matthews said. "Although they remain individual pieces of paper, a bond is formed between them and they become one. If you take them apart, pieces of one will remain on the other, and neither piece will ever be the same. Every person with whom you have sexual intimacy alters something in your spirit or soul. You are forever changed! Although we don't know the full impact this has on us, if we believe the Bible we must accept that sexual intercourse has serious consequences. It's of no wonder the Bible speaks against sex outside of marriage. Even a casual sexual encounter changes us."

David, not being a Christian, wasn't sure what he could take from these Bible statements, but for some reason a deep truth resonated in these words.

They also discussed the topic of effective listening. Matthews pointed out that listening involves more than being quiet. It requires that we surrender our preoccupation with self in order to enter into another's experience.

"This means that our focus needs to be on understanding the other person rather than validating our own thoughts, feelings, and beliefs," he said. "You need to have the mindset to understand as much as possible about the speaker and their situation without judging, condemning, or comparing."

There was also a session on exploring the power of silence. In one exercise, each couple sat on the floor, back to back, while contemplating various aspects of their marriage. David was surprised how effective this exercise was. As his back touched Deborah's, he remembered the phrase "The two become one."

They were given a mind-boggling abundance of information. David wondered how he would ever process all this material—and more importantly, apply it. So he was very pleased to hear

Mathews say that the seminar fee included online access to the organization's website, where they could get continuous help in understanding and implementing the material.

By the time the session ended, they were ready to break for the day. The couples were all ushered into the room they'd had dinner in the night before. David and Deborah's new table companions were a couple from Raleigh, North Carolina. They had a great conversation over lunch.

By one o'clock, David and Deborah left on a tour of historic St. Augustine. David had booked the tour to give them an overview of the area, as they had planned to spend a few extra days exploring the city after the seminar was over.

CHAPTER FIFTEEN

Diary Entry, May 29, 2013

Thought of the day: We seldom embrace change until the cost of staying as we are is greater than the cost to change.

It's always nice to get back home, but what a wonderful time I had in St. Augustine. The city is so rich in history and architecture. Places such as Flagler College and the Lightner Museum were incredibly beautiful. We took a unique walking tour that incorporated both history and food. We sampled clam chowder, wine smoothies, exceptional baked products, a Reuben roll, Oyster Meehan, and various wines and teas. All of this, plus we learned a lot about history. It doesn't get much better than that!

The marriage seminar exceeded all my expectations and gave me new optimism about our marriage. I have identified many things I can do to make our marriage better. I'm looking forward to building a new, deeper intimacy with Deborah. I realize now that I had been heading for serious trouble.

I need to bring Catherine and my relationship back to its proper place. It will likely make things difficult for a while, but I'm hoping we can overcome this and continue with a good business relationship.

———

THE FIRST CHANGE DEBORAH AND DAVID DECIDED UPON WAS TO make an effort to spend more time together. They planned to have breakfast together at the start of each day.

On their first morning, Deborah told David that she would be handing down a verdict on the age discrimination case that day. David looked straight into her eyes and truly listened to what she said. He realized the immense pressure Deborah worked under. Her decisions could seriously impact the future of many people. He was proud of his wife and the important work she did, and for the first time he told her so. Deborah thanked him and asked about his plans for the day.

He told Deborah he wasn't sure what to expect, as this was the first time Catherine had been left alone to run the office. He mentioned nothing to Deborah about the talk he would have with Catherine relating to the changes that needed to be made in their relationship. In fact, David decided not to tell Deborah anything about what had transpired between him and Catherine. In this case, he doubted that honesty was the best policy.

With breakfast over, they said their goodbyes, kissed, and went their separate ways.

As Deborah drove to work, she pondered how, over the course of the trial, she had been alerted to the staggering impact aging had on people. The case had shown her how aging could affect work, and the marriage seminar had opened her eyes to the affects aging had on marriages.

Until this case had come up, she hadn't thought much about the effects of aging other than the odd time when she looked in the mirror and saw a wrinkle staring back at her or found a gray hair. However, it seemed age-related topics were popping up at every turn of late. In the last while, she had heard a steady stream of news stories relating to age. Lifespan was increasing and this aging would likely place a great burden on society, fueling discrimination.

When Deborah entered the courtroom to read her verdict, she was surprised at how many people, including reporters, were in attendance. Her verdict would no doubt be on the evening news. People would discuss the verdict around the water cooler.

Deborah noticed that the elderly gentleman with the penetrating eyes sat in the gallery.

"The plaintiff has proven beyond a reasonable doubt that his client was capable of doing her job," Deborah began. "This was attested to by two pieces of evidence: first, the amount of tips earned, and second, the letter from her current employer. The defendant has failed to provide proof that his reason for terminating Ms. Curte was on any ground other than her age."

Deborah went on to explain that if the action taken by the defendant had been taken because of ethnicity rather than age, society's alarm would have quickly sounded. But age discrimination was still in its infancy; therefore incidents could slip by without notice.

She turned and looked directly at Ms. Curte. "I commend Ms. Curte for her courage to stand up for what she believed to be right, and I find for the plaintiff in the amount of fifty thousand dollars."

With the drop of her gavel, she declared, "Court is adjourned."

Dennis chuckled to himself as he heard the verdict. He realized that Judge MacDonald's verdict had condemned her husband for choosing a younger partner. Surely that was a form of age discrimination. However, in David's case, Dennis would be the one to decide on the penalty—and he would enjoy watching it unfold.

CHAPTER SIXTEEN

DAVID'S DAY DIDN'T UNFOLD ACCORDING TO PLAN. HE CHANGED HIS mind and decided not to directly confront Catherine with the change in their relationship. He feared looking like a fool if he had misread her signals.

His return from the seminar provided an excellent starting point from which to convince Catherine how dedicated he was to Deborah and what a great marriage they had. Perhaps if Catherine had any thoughts of kindling a romantic relationship with him, this would be enough to let her know it was not to be.

The conference had significantly changed his attitude toward his marriage and provided the tools he needed to deal with his feelings of inadequacy brought on by aging. He was confident he wouldn't have a problem working with Catherine and maintaining his professionalism.

David and Catherine started their day in the customary fashion of having their morning coffee and discussion. David took advantage of this time to tell her about the conference, emphasizing how much he had enjoyed spending time with Deborah and how good they were together.

He then jumped directly from that topic to business.

Catherine reported that everything had gone well in his absence and she had no outstanding issues to discuss. David looked at the summary she handed him, and after a quick review he commended her performance. His first instinct was to take her out for lunch to thank her, but he realized that wasn't a good idea. He would plan a more formal way to reward her for her excellent work.

Although David's message was subtle, Catherine heard it loud and clear. When Catherine returned home from work, the pressure of having worked the whole day pretending everything was okay, when in fact everything had changed, left her angry and feeling sorry for herself. She needed a night out to relieve her tension and drown her sorrows. Having no circle of friends, she purposed to go out and have a nice meal, then go to a bar. She was very confident in her ability to meet someone to distract her from the day's events.

Before getting ready to go out, she poured herself a drink and took solace by emailing Lisa. Typing out her fantasy, she recounted to Lisa how David had missed her so much while he was away with his wife. She then wrote that they'd had sex on his office couch before even finishing their morning coffee. Her email went on to report that David had told her he was now absolutely sure he and Deborah should separate; he wanted to make a life with Catherine. This would all take time, but they would eventually be together. It would be easier for everyone concerned, wrote Catherine, if Deborah had an accident and died. One could only hope!

———

When Dennis intercepted Catherine's email and read it, he was furious. The time for planning was over; it was now time to make David pay!

Dennis went to his home office and completed the work he had started on the Photoshopped images he'd made of David and Catherine making love. He selected five of the best shots and prepared them to be sent to Judge MacDonald.

He drove four hours from his home to mail the pictures so there would be no possibility of tracing them to him. Later he called David's office to make an appointment for the next day. He said that he'd come into a sizeable inheritance and wanted to talk about investment possibilities.

Dennis then turned his attention to his surveillance of Catherine's apartment. She was soaking in her tub, trying to relax from her difficult day. He marveled at her beauty. Yet here he was again, at the point in the relationship of needing to end it. He watched as she got out of the tub and toweled herself dry; he was disappointed such a beauty had to die.

He turned off the monitor. "See you soon, my love."

Dennis sat back with his hands joined behind his neck, mentally reviewing his plan. Everything was in place; there would be no way out. The evidence against David would be so compelling that even David's best friends would believe he was guilty.

Not only would the revenge be sweet, observing the process would be a fascinating study in human nature. Dennis suspected David had up until now lived a clean, respectful life. But because of one indiscretion, he would be crucified. When the time came, people would turn against him in an instant, especially those who were closest to him.

How would Deborah deal with all this? Would her analytical and fair mind be overcome by emotions, or would she be strong enough to give David the benefit of the doubt?

Dennis roared with laughter. *You'll find out there is no such thing as friendship, Mr. MacDonald. You'll be hung out to dry.*

———

The next day, a little hung over, Catherine got ready for work and started the first part of her plan to win back David's affections. Her office dress so far had been rather conservative, but now she felt she needed to make a change. A new look was required, one that was sexy but still classy. Her father had often told her she was an incredibly beautiful young lady and there was no reason not to use all her assets to get what she wanted. She so much missed having her father in her life.

During Catherine and David's morning coffee together, she sensed that David had noticed and was enjoying her new look. He was obviously trying not to get caught staring; each time she turned to him, he quickly looked away. She was confident that her plan was working.

As they finished coffee and prepared to work, she discussed with David the message Mr. Cain had left. They managed to fit him into the day's schedule.

———

When Dennis received Catherine's call to book his appointment, he was excited to hear her voice. She had a way about her that made even a business conversation an enjoyable experience. As Dennis hung up, his mind was already imagining what she would be wearing and how beautiful she would look.

When he arrived at the office, Dennis was not disappointed. Catherine's welcoming smile lit up the entire room. She wore a beige blouse with a plunging neckline. The blouse was gathered under a wide black belt into a snug skirt that accentuated her tiny waist and beautiful legs. As he drew near, he was seduced by the wonderful scent of her perfume.

"Please have a seat," Catherine said. "Mr. MacDonald will be out shortly. Could I get you a coffee?"

"Yes, please."

"If I remember right, you take it black."

"Yes." Dennis was thrilled she remembered.

When she bent over to serve his coffee, his eyes feasted on her. He almost forgot to say thank you.

Dennis only had a few sips of his coffee before David came out to greet him and usher him into his office.

It almost annoyed Dennis that, despite all that had happened, he still liked David. How could he hate and like someone at the same time?

Dennis explained that he had received a six-figure inheritance that needed to be invested. He went on to say that he had a friend who was looking for a silent partner in a new business that would manufacture and distribute 3D printers.

"I'm seeking your advice," Dennis said. "Would I be better to invest this money through you, or do you believe this business could be a good opportunity?"

"You're already in a commendable position so far as your retirement fund is concerned," David pointed out. "Perhaps this need not be an either/or decision. You could invest in your friend's business to the extent you feel comfortable, thinking of the inheritance as found money. The remainder could be allocated to options such as a charitable trust."

Dennis was impressed. David seemed to really want the best for him and wasn't hedging toward what would bring in the biggest fee.

"I appreciate the advice," Dennis said. "I'll get back to you once I consider all the options." He then asked David to photocopy the information he had shown him about charitable trusts.

Dennis knew from his previous visit that David would leave his office to take the photocopies. While David was away, Dennis completed the last part of his plan.

Upon David's return, Dennis thanked him for his time, picked up his photocopies, and left. He went directly to Catherine's desk to thank her for the coffee. Once again he basked in the joy of being near her.

CHAPTER SEVENTEEN

Diary Entry, June 5, 2013

Thought of the day: Rhythm and harmony, what beautiful words they are; paired together in the dance of love they lead to exhilarated peace.

Ever since the marriage seminar, Deborah and I have reclaimed our relationship; I feel like I'm in love again. We have been spending much more time together and enjoying each other's company.

Last Sunday, we went to the church Paul was preaching at and he did a fabulous job. His topic was, how do we know who's a Christian? I love his ability to simplify things that seem so complicated. His question requires one to identify what is a Christian, and he answered with this simple answer: "A Christian is one who believes that Jesus was indeed the Messiah that the world had been waiting for, and He is the only way to eternal life with God." Christians believe this to such an extent that they commit to following Jesus. This is the way of love—the love of God and the love of others.

As I've been spending more time talking with Deborah about Christianity, I'm starting to see how different it is to what I grew up believing. So many people are searching far eastern

religions or seeking new age wisdom while they ignore the teach-
ings of Christ, which have been tried and proven over and over
again. Look at Canada and the United States: two countries
built on Christian teachings. They are two of the best countries
in the world. Our forefathers didn't get it all right, but in spite of
their humanness they still achieved remarkable results. Unfortu-
nately, as our country moves away from its Christian heritage,
problems are arising that seem almost insurmountable.

I've decided that I want to seriously investigate what Chris-
tianity is all about. Paul and Deborah have made me aware that
there's a big difference between what Jesus taught and how that
has been distorted by religious people shaping those teachings for
their own purposes. According to Paul, religion is man's under-
standing and response to life; Christianity is God's revelation,
through Jesus and the Bible, of why we are here and where we're
going. I want to try to remove all the preconceived ideas I have
about Christianity and just go and study the teachings of Jesus.

———

DAVID PUT AWAY HIS DIARY AND WENT TO WORK. LATELY HE'D HAD SO
much on his mind that he was having difficulty focusing on the
routine things of life, but on this day, mercifully, his day passed
quickly. He was excited about meeting up with Paul for dinner,
anxious to tell him all about the marriage seminar.

David had picked the restaurant. What made this place different was that you had to have a reservation and choose at the time
of reservation one of four meals being offered. The efficiency of
preparing only food that would be served allowed the restaurant to
serve high-quality food for a very economical price.

He arrived before Paul and ordered a pinot noir from a winery
located only a short jaunt down the highway in Beamsville. He'd
no sooner sipped his wine when Paul arrived. On David's recom-
mendation, Paul ordered a glass of the same wine.

David was excited to tell him what a difference the seminar had made in his marriage. He recounted how meeting Al and Dolores Freeman had helped him to realize that he and Deborah had felt a void as they came to the end of accomplishing their life goals. He had felt lost. The seminar had provided many useful teachings and tools to help them move through this new phase.

Paul smiled, pleased that things had gone so well. David admired how Paul genuinely cared for others and celebrated in their joy.

Paul's face lit up as he proclaimed that he, too, had good news. "I have applied for a position of lead pastor at a church not far from here. I was notified today that the interview went well and they want me to preach at a service. This is done so the board of elders can see how the congregation responds to me."

David frowned and tilted his head. "I didn't realize you had resolved the issues that kept you away from ministry."

"I'm not completely sure I have, but I felt God leading me to apply for this position. I figured if I got the position, God would take care of the rest. For the most part I've simply been dealing with the question of why bad things happen to good people. I've come to grips with that and I'm ready to move on."

"Interesting." David leaned forward and sipped his wine. "Tell me, why do bad things happen to good people?"

"The short answer is that we're all sinners and live in a world full of sin. What we call bad things are actually the consequences of sin. What often confuses people is that the consequences of sin don't only fall on the sinner; they fall on others as well. Therefore, when we see something bad happen to someone who didn't seem to deserve it, we question why."

David crossed his arms in front of him. "I'm missing something here."

"Okay, let me give you an example," Paul replied. "A drunk driver who hits and kills a child will suffer some consequences for his sinfulness, but so too will the child and his family. The child did nothing to deserve being hit by a car but suffered the consequences brought on by the actions of the drunk driver. The consequences that fall on a person may in fact have nothing to do with their own actions, but those consequences still originate from sin and not from God."

David shook his head. "I thought Jesus' forgiveness of sin protected Christians from the consequences of sin, but obviously not. So what does it do?"

Paul smiled. "Sin has a spiritual consequence, which is to separate us from God, but it also has worldly consequences. A Christian's sin is forgiven, removing the spiritual consequence so he is not separated from God. However the worldly consequences most often remain. Those who choose to make righteous choices in dealing with these consequences can overcome them and transform them into something good. For those who choose to wallow in self-pity and focus on how unfair their situation is, they will remain in the mire of the consequences."

"I think I get it now. We're looking for a direct consequence to sin when many times it's not evident. Rather than focusing on whose fault it is, we should turn our attention to overcoming the consequences."

"Right," said Paul. "I've got a question for you now."

"What's that?"

"Have you noticed that as the time nears for us to go work on my car, you always seem to come up with heavy questions? Might that be procrastination?

They laughed as David put his hand over his heart. "I'm hurt that you think I'd do such a thing."

CHAPTER EIGHTEEN

Diary Entry, June 6, 2013

Thought of the day: I hate change, but I love variety.

Not too long ago, I was feeling like life had passed me by. I had it all, but in a way I had nothing at all. How quickly things can change. Today I feel like life is good. The sun is shining and the weather forecast is for a beautiful week.

I had a great time with Paul last night and I'm thrilled he is making the big change of going back into ministry. I sensed, as he spoke with me, that this is where he was truly meant to be. Work consumes so much of one's time; we need to be doing something we feel is at least enjoyable if not purposeful. I expect I'm going to see a new Paul, one who is passionate about his accomplishments and excited about the future.

The teaching I took away from the marriage conference, to focus on personal change rather than changing others, is radical. Why shouldn't we always focus on wanting to be our best regardless of what others do? Life truly is a mirror. What you put in front of it is what will reflect back to you.

Deborah and I are in our twenty-fifth year of marriage and I'm excited about the date night we have planned for Friday evening. Life is so good!

WHEN DAVID ARRIVED AT WORK, HE WAS SURPRISED CATHERINE wasn't there. She always opened the office and had coffee waiting for him. In her absence, he decided to put on the coffee. He listened to the messages while it brewed. There was no message from Catherine indicating she would be late.

He let an hour pass before he decided to call Catherine to see what was happening. The phone rang and rang but there was no answer. This was so unlike Catherine. As her parents were both dead and she had no siblings, there was no one he could contact. He had no pending appointments scheduled, so he decided to close the office and go to her apartment to check on her.

He buzzed her apartment but received no answer. He then buzzed Mrs. Field, the superintendent. She remembered him from the night he'd had dinner at Catherine's.

David explained his concern and they went together to Catherine's apartment. After calling Catherine's name several times, Mrs. Field unlocked the door and called out, "Super. Are you here, Catherine?"

David followed her into the apartment. The apartment was tidy and did not suggest anything unusual. He suggested that Mrs. Field check the bedroom while he checked the bathroom. She tapped lightly on the door, calling Catherine's name. Receiving no response, she pushed open the door and peeked her head in.

Her scream was so loud that David came running. As he raced through the door, he saw Catherine's blood-soaked nude body on the bed. Both he and Mrs. Field turned in horror and left the room.

David used his cell phone to call 911. As he spoke to the operator, he felt he was going to vomit. The minute he was off the phone he ran to the bathroom and upchucked into the toilet. Once he composed himself and returned to the living room, he saw Mrs. Field sitting on the couch, her face as white as a sheet. David told her that the police were on the way.

They decided to go to the lobby to wait for the responders. They didn't have to wait long before they heard sirens blaring; police, ambulance, and even a fire truck pulled up in front of the building. People gathered, anxious to find out what was happening. Mrs. Field and David led the responders to Catherine's apartment.

After establishing the nature of the emergency, the police told Mrs. Field to go and tell the residents they didn't have to evacuate the building. They cautioned her not to say anything other than that there had been a death in one of the apartments.

The police contacted the coroner's office, then turned their attention to asking David about his relationship to the deceased woman. They documented his personal information, collected information pertaining to Catherine, and asked him to wait in the lobby until the detectives arrived and had a chance to speak with him.

David returned to the lobby and sat on the couch. He was in a fog, unable to process what had happened. He was trembling and he felt cold. He didn't know what to do next.

As he tried to pull himself together, a man approached and introduced himself as Detective Richardson. He sat on the couch beside David. "How are you doing?"

"I think I'm still in shock."

"Do you feel you could answer some questions for me?"

"I'll do my best."

"I would like to drive you and Mrs. Field to the station so we can get your statement while it's fresh in your mind," Richardson said. "Once we're done, an officer will return you to pick up your car. Will that be all right with you?

"Yes."

When they arrived at the station, Richardson's partner took Mrs. Field into one interview room and he ushered David into another.

"I have closed the door for privacy reasons, but I want you to know that you are free to leave at any point through this interview," Richardson said. "We are trying to get more information so we can understand the events surrounding the death of Ms. Catherine Boudreau. This interview will be videotaped to provide an accurate record of what is said. Do you understand all of this, Mr. MacDonald?"

"Yes, I do."

"Good, then let's get started. Mr. MacDonald, tell me what led to you and Mrs. Field finding Ms. Boudreau."

"Catherine is my secretary, and when I got to the office this morning she had not yet arrived. This was the first time since her hiring she had been late. I checked the messages to see if she had called. There was no message from her, so I presumed she would be in shortly and proceeded to make coffee and get started with my day."

"How long had she worked for you?"

"Approximately six months."

"Tell me about your relationship with her."

"We got along quite well. She was a very efficient secretary, extremely well organized, and as I've already indicated, very dependable."

"Explain what happened as your day went on."

"After she was more than an hour late, I called her and there was no answer. So I went to her place to check on her."

"You just closed up your office and left?"

"Yes. I had no appointments scheduled and there was no one else I could call to check on her."

"You had no person to contact in case of emergency listed in your personnel files?"

"No, I did not. Catherine had told me that her parents had died in a car accident a few years ago. She had no next of kin that I knew about."

"Go on. Explain what happened next."

"When I got to Catherine's building and buzzed her apartment, I got no answer, so I pressed the button for the superintendent and explained the situation. She buzzed me in and met me in the lobby. We proceeded together to Catherine's apartment. Mrs. Field knocked on the door several times and there was no response. She unlocked the door and we both entered."

"Describe what you saw."

"The apartment is not very big, so I could see at a glance all the rooms except for the bathroom and the bedroom. After we called out to Catherine a few more times, I suggested Mrs. Field check the bedroom and I would go check the bathroom. As I approached the bathroom, I heard a piercing scream from Mrs. Field and ran to her."

"Tell me what you saw."

"It was gruesome. Catherine was lying on the bed and her neck had been cut. There was blood all over the bed."

"What did you think had happened?"

"I didn't think. I just ran from the bedroom, called 911, and headed for the bathroom because I was afraid I was going to be sick to my stomach."

"I know this is difficult for you, Mr. MacDonald. You're doing great."

"As soon as I could compose myself, I suggested to Mrs. Field that we go to the lobby to wait for the responders to arrive."

"Then what happened?"

"Mrs. Field and I left the apartment and went to the lobby to wait."

"What can you tell me about Catherine?"

"I've told you all I know about her."

"Describe your relationship with her."

"I was her employer. We had a normal work relationship."

"Did you have discussions with her about her friends?"

"No, I did not."

"What do you believe happened to Ms. Boudreau?"

"I have no idea."

"Is there anything more you can tell me that may help me get to the bottom of what happened?"

"No."

"Thank you for your help, Mr. MacDonald, and if you should come up with anything else, here's my card. Please call. I have your contact information in my file and I'll call you if we have further questions."

Richardson called an officer to give David a ride back to the apartment building. He shook David's hand as they parted.

When they arrived at the apartment building, David left the police car and got into his own car to drive back to his office. He couldn't believe what had transpired.

Things like this don't happen to people like me, he thought. *This is the worst day of my life.*

He took care of the essentials at the office before closing up. He knew he was going to need a few days before he was ready to do any business, so he stopped off at the security office on his way out to advise them that his office would be closed for a few days.

He decided not to call Deborah with the news; something like this needed to be discussed face to face. He felt he needed her presence and looked forward to being held by her, to draw on her strength and be comforted in his time of need.

———

Deborah was home enjoying her day off by doing some gardening. By midday, she was hungry and decided to stop for some lunch. She cut some slices of cheese and put out some crackers to enjoy with the homemade soup a friend had given her.

She remembered the large envelope in the morning mail addressed to her. Curious, she got the mail and opened the large envelope. She was stunned as she looked through the contents, her eyes falling upon nude pictures of David and his secretary in compromising positions. The note with the pictures was made up of letters cut from a magazine: "I thought you should know."

Deborah was furious. Immediately she called David's office only to hear a recording saying that the office was closed so please leave a message. Deborah slammed the phone down and screamed in frustration. Looking down at the pictures, she suddenly realized one of them had been taken in her bedroom. How could David have done this to her?

Just then, she heard a car coming up the drive. Running to the window, she saw that it was David. She gathered the pictures in her hand and waited for him to come through the door. When he came, she tossed them in his face and stomped off to the bedroom, slamming the door and locking it.

———

David picked up the pictures, horrified by what he saw. What was happening? Was he in a nightmare? Where had these come from?

He called after Deborah and begged her to open the door but she did not even respond. "Deborah, these pictures aren't true. I don't know where they came from, but I can assure you they have to be doctored. I have never been unfaithful to you."

"How would anyone have nude pictures of you and a picture of the inside of our bedroom?" screamed Deborah. "How could you do this to me? Was the marriage seminar your attempt to convince me you cared, or was it your subconscious way of telling me our marriage was over?"

"Deborah, I know how bad this looks, but I'm as confused about all this as you are. This day has been crazy! Catherine has been murdered." He told her the story of discovering the body. "I need you to believe me, Deborah. I'm living a nightmare!"

David heard the door unlock and Deborah stepped out of the bedroom. He reached out to hug her, but she stepped away from him.

"Don't touch me," she said. "There are too many unanswered questions. I can't put all this aside and go on as if nothing has happened."

"I understand how this must look to you."

"No, you don't. You don't understand anything about me. You don't understand how betrayed I feel. I trusted you and now I wonder if I ever really knew you."

David felt ready to scream. Although he could understand how bad this looked, he felt that she should give him more consideration given their twenty-five years together. Why was she so willing to believe the worst about him? He held his emotions in check, not wanting to make matters worse.

Deborah gathered some clothes and headed for the guest bedroom. "After seeing those pictures, there's no way I can sleep in our bed. You can sleep wherever you want, so long as it's not in the same room as me."

David didn't know what to do or think. He sat on the floor, looking at the pictures, and began to sob. Although his confusion over the pictures weighed heavily, the vivid memory of Catherine covered in blood so horrified him that his whole body convulsed. Neither his body nor his mind knew how to process what he had witnessed. He couldn't handle this alone and Deborah clearly wasn't going to be any help.

As he sat in a daze, the only person he could think to call was Paul.

He went into the den, dialed Paul's number, and repeated the phrase, "Pick up!"

Finally, Paul answered.

"Paul, it's David. I have a serious situation and I need someone to talk with. Do you have some time?"

Paul could hear the anxiety in David's voice and sensed his desperation. "Where are you now?"

"I'm at home," David replied.

"I'm leaving now. I should be there in ten minutes. Will you be all right until I get there?"

"Yes, thank you so much. I really appreciate this."

"Okay, buddy. I'm on my way."

With that, Paul hung up the phone, ran to his car, and drove away.

When Paul arrived, David was sitting on the back step and looked terrible. Paul walked directly to him and hugged him without saying a word. David didn't resist this unusual greeting. It was exactly what he needed.

As they stepped apart, David told him what had happened at Catherine's apartment and then what happened when he got home.

"Wow!" Paul said. "No wonder you're upset. Where is Deborah now?"

"In the guest bedroom with the door shut. She won't speak with me. I can see how bad this looks, but I swear, Paul, I didn't do what's depicted in these pictures. You've got to believe me."

"I do believe you, David."

"Thank you so much, Paul. You don't know how much that means to me. What am I going to do?"

"Let's take this one step at a time. Let me go see if Deborah is all right and if she will talk with me."

"Thank you."

Paul went into the house. When he reached the guest bedroom, he knocked gently on the door. "Deborah, it's Paul Evans. Will you open the door so we can talk?"

He heard her footsteps coming toward the door, and when she opened it the tears were streaming down her cheeks. He reached out and let her walk into his arms. He held her as she broke down and cried. When the sobbing finally stopped, she told Paul how betrayed she felt.

"How could he do this to me?" she asked.

"I don't have any answers for you, Deborah. I can only suggest at times like these, when nothing makes sense, that we need to lean on God. Could I pray with you? "

"Yes. But can I ask you a question first? And will you promise to answer truthfully?"

"Certainly."

"Has David quite often met with you to work on your car or was he using that to cover up meeting with Catherine?"

"David and I have often had dinner together and afterward went to work on the car."

"You must think I'm heartless, not showing any concern for what has happened to Catherine."

"No, I don't. I saw the pictures and they are very disturbing. You have every right to be upset and focused on what this means to you. Let's pray and ask for God's help."

They bowed their heads and Paul prayed, "Lord, help us to get to the bottom of all that has happened. Let us not judge before we have all the facts. Empower us to trust You and rely on Your strength to carry us through this. Amen."

"Thanks so much, Paul, for being here for us. I know David and I need to talk through this, but I'm so angry that I don't even want to be in the same room with him. However, if you can stay and facilitate for us, I'll try to pull myself together and come out to join you and David in a little while. Can you stay?"

"I'm here for as long as you need me. I'll go back out with David and you come when you're ready."

Paul returned to the living room and sat with David. He told David that he would have to be patient with Deborah. They needed to deal with the issue of the pictures before they could address his feelings concerning the traumatic experience he had been through.

David agreed with Paul's assessment and knew he had to put Deborah's feelings first.

While they waited for Deborah to join them, David put on some coffee.

"Do you have any idea how the pictures were produced?" David asked.

"With the technology of the day, pictures are easily manipulated. But I don't know enough about the science of it to have any idea how it's done."

"What really troubles me is the rooms they take place in are either here in our house or at Catherine's apartment. Where did the raw data come from to manipulate these pictures? I've never taken a nude picture of myself and I certainly have never been in the nude together with Catherine."

Just then, Deborah walked into the room. She picked up the last part of the conversation. "You already know what I think about these pictures," she said, "but I wonder if you realize that if these pictures were also sent to the police, they would provide strong circumstantial evidence to link you, by motive, to Catherine's murder."

David's face paled as he stared into nothingness. "Oh my God, you're right! These make me a prime suspect. This day keeps getting worse and worse."

"Calm down," said Paul. "Let's not get too far ahead of ourselves. With your legal experience, Deborah, would you recommend David should contact a lawyer?"

"Divorce or criminal?" replied Deborah. "I'm sorry. I'm still having trouble dealing with my anger. There's not much point in contacting a lawyer until the police indicate whether David is a person of interest." She turned to David. "Have you been interviewed by the police yet?"

"Yes. They interviewed me at the police station before I came home, but they only asked general questions and told me they would call if they had further questions."

"That would suggest they haven't yet seen these pictures, Deborah said. "Will there be other incriminating evidence for them to uncover, such as motel rooms booked, places you may have been seen together, etc.?"

"Deborah, I never did anything wrong with Catherine. But as these pictures so aptly prove, one can be made to look guilty even when they're not. I've been out on occasion for lunch with her, and on one occasion I went to her apartment to help her fix her computer. Unbeknownst to me, she had fixed an extravagant dinner. I didn't tell you. I know I should have, but I promise you nothing happened."

"I seem to remember an American president saying, 'I did not have sex with that woman.' And we all know how that turned out."

"If I can't convince you of my innocence after living with you the past twenty-five years, what hope do I have if I get charged for Catherine's murder?"

Deborah sighed. "Oh what a tangled web we weave—"

Paul interrupted to refocus them on the problem at hand. "Do either of you know if there's a service available to have your house swept for bugs and hidden cameras? It seems to me this would be a logical way for someone to get pictures."

"That's a great suggestion." said David. "I'll see what's available, and if so, how soon it can be done."

"Do you actually believe someone may be spying on us in our own home?" asked Deborah.

"Those pictures had to be obtained somehow," Paul said. "Giving David the benefit of the doubt, that seems to be the most logical explanation." He then suggested it would be wise if they took time to settle their emotions.

Deborah and David agreed and thanked Paul for coming over.

After Paul left, Deborah told David she would wait until some of these issues could be resolved before she took any action concerning their relationship. Until then, she would sleep in the guest bedroom and expect him to respect her privacy. She walked back to the bedroom and shut the door.

David poured himself a glass of wine and sat in the den, his mind scarcely able to process what he had experienced this day.

When he had awakened that morning, he had been heading for what he thought was going to be a wonderful day. Everything in his life had been going better than ever before. He had finally been starting to feel complete. His talks with Paul and the marriage seminar had led him to believe in and want a relationship with God. Just as he had started pursuing God, it seemed God slapped him in the face—and hit him hard!

Perhaps he deserved it, yet somehow he felt betrayed. He remembered how Deborah had expressed her feelings of betrayal. He had some sense of how unfair all this must seem to her. In her eyes, he had rejected twenty-five years of her love and laughed about it behind her back.

The reality that Deborah might leave him sunk into his consciousness. As angry as he was with God, he felt he had no alternative but to pray to Him for help.

CHAPTER NINETEEN

WHEN DAVID AWAKENED THE NEXT MORNING, HE KEPT HIS EYES shut while his mind processed what he remembered. He prayed that once he opened his eyes, he would find that all the events of yesterday had only been a bad dream. He slowly opened his eyes and observed that he was indeed in the den and still fully dressed. Yesterday had really happened.

Although he didn't feel up to writing his daily diary entry, he decided it may help him to process all that had taken place.

———

Diary Entry, June 7, 2013

Thought of the day: If we don't learn from the storms of life, the tragedy is compounded.

Where do I start to describe my day? The first thought that comes to mind is the book my dad used to read to me when I was a child: Alexander and the Terrible, Horrible, No Good, Very Bad Day. That title sums it up.

I can't believe Catherine is dead and the horror that ended her life. I will never be able to get that picture out of my mind. There must be some connection between the pictures Deborah was sent and Catherine's death. It's too big of a coincidence for these two events not to be related.

What is the perpetrator trying to accomplish? The only logical possibility in my mind is that I'm being framed for murder. But why? Why would anyone want to murder Catherine? Was there some deep dark secret I didn't know about? Whatever the reason, I'm terrified; the evidence has already convinced Deborah I'm guilty. Would another judge not come to the same conclusion? I can only hope that when I have the house swept for bugs, that will prove someone has been gathering the images required to Photoshop the pictures. I can also hope the police don't have the pictures, but that seems highly unlikely.

I have to get my day started, but I'd rather curl up and disappear.

———

David found several companies that offered counter surveillance, electronic debugging, technical security services. He scheduled an appointment for the work to be performed that same day.

He heard Deborah making coffee in the kitchen and was unsure how to greet her. It felt so strange not to know how to greet his own wife.

He proceeded to the kitchen. "Good morning."

"Good morning," Deborah murmured, but she quickly turned away.

David poured himself a coffee. "Could you somehow find the strength to give me the same benefit you would give an accused in your courtroom? Would you consider that I might be innocent until some guilt is proven?"

"That is exactly what I'm doing, otherwise we wouldn't be under the same roof. The problem right now is we can't risk having the pictures analyzed for authenticity until we know if the police have copies, and I'm having difficulty understanding how these pictures could be Photoshopped. Where did someone get pictures of our bedroom and your nude body?"

"I understand your confusion. I don't know how it's possible either."

He realized that so much depended on what the surveillance company found.

He returned to the den to call Edith Bickle. He needed someone to manage the office until he could go back to work, until he could hire someone to replace Catherine. Edith was the best choice, if there was any chance she was willing to return to work.

———

When Edith Bickle answered the phone, she immediately recognized his voice. "It so nice to hear from you."

"You may change your mind after I tell you why I've called." He went on to recount the happenings of Catherine's murder and to ask if there was any possibility she would be available to help him out.

Edith was shocked by the account of Catherine's death and agreed to fill in.

David explained it might be a few days before he could come to work again. He thanked Edith and advised her that he would call security and authorize them to open the office for her.

Although Edith was saddened by the news of Catherine's tragic death, she was excited to be heading back to the office she had managed for so many years.

———

David looked down at the clothes he was wearing, which he had slept in all night, and decided it was time to clean up.

David stepped into the spa shower and pushed a button. As he plopped himself down on a bench, he melted into a soothing cloud of eucalyptus-scented steam. He tried to clear his mind, relax, and shake off the stress of the past few days. Although he had enjoyed the spa shower before, it never felt as good as it did this day. He sat there for the longest time, not wanting to face his troubles. Finally he switched off the steam and turned on the multi-jet shower to receive a therapeutic massage. He pampered himself for a little longer, then finally stepped out, hopeful things would take a turn for the better.

He dressed and grabbed a coffee. As the grandfather clock struck eleven o'clock, David heard a vehicle come up the drive.

The driver introduced himself to David and explained that the company's vans carried no markings for confidentiality reasons. He told David he would do some external checks of all entry points to the house. Next he would come inside to check for bugs, cameras, and run a complete check of all the computers in the house.

David felt confident as he watched the man test lines, search for pinholes with high-intensity light, and investigate countless other details. Throughout the process, David had the feeling he knew this man but he couldn't recall from where.

After two hours of work, the security man reported that he hadn't found any evidence that the house had been tampered with.

David was very disappointed with the results. He worried that not sharing information about the pictures (such as that they depicted the bedroom) may have tainted the security man's ability to provide the answers David was looking for, but he felt he had to keep that information to himself.

———

As the van drove away, Dennis Cain roared with laughter, proud that his disguise had successfully fooled David. His plan to have routing control over the outgoing calls on David's phone had truly been a work of art. To be invited into the house so he could set everything back to normal testified to his genius.

———

David reluctantly knocked on the guest bedroom door to let Deborah know the sweep had not revealed any evidence of tampering. Deborah didn't answer and David went back to the den.

A little while later, Deborah came into the den holding two cups of coffee. She handed one to David. "What do we do now?"

"I really don't know."

He finished his coffee with Deborah as they both sat in a daze, not knowing how to deal with the hand they had been dealt. Their silence was broken by the chime of the doorbell.

David opened the door and was surprised to see Detective Richardson standing before him with an army of other officers. The detective told him he was there to execute a search warrant to seize computers and other electronic devices used to communicate, store, or transmit electronic data. The warrant also covered David's office and cars.

David was shocked by this turn of events. His mind raced, trying to remember where he had last put the pictures. Why had he not thought to get rid of them? Desperation flooded him, his head ached, and his muscles tensed. All warmth left his body. It was all he could do not to break down crying like an abandoned child. He had never felt as alone as he did now. Hopeless, beaten down, and defenseless, he robotically held the door open while the multitude of officers entered his home.

He went to the couch and sat beside Deborah as the police carried out their search. Deborah told him he shouldn't answer any more questions before he talked with a lawyer, and if they charged him with an offence she would call a friend who was a criminal lawyer.

"Detective, I think you will want to see this."

The words rang in David's consciousness, a clamorous sound that deafened everything else.

Before long, Detective Richardson entered the living room holding the pictures.

"You are not under arrest, but you're being detained for questioning," Richardson said. "You have the right to legal counsel. Do you understand?"

"Yes, I do."

When they arrived at the police station, Richardson led David down the hall to the same interview room they had used previously.

"These pictures I'm holding in my hands suggest there are some parts of our previous discussion I need to have clarified," Richardson said, sitting down in the chair across the table. "You told me your only relationship to Ms. Boudreau was that of employer/employee. Is that correct?

"I have been advised to not answer any questions until I retain a lawyer."

"You do have the right to not speak, Mr. MacDonald, but it's obvious from the facts we have uncovered that you care about Ms. Boudreau, and I'm sure you want us to get to the bottom of what happened to her. So let me tell you how this looks from my perspective. You are a highly successful man and can enjoy the finer things in life. You hire a new employee, who by your own account turns out to be an excellent worker. We know you have visited her apartment. Ms. Boudreau herself told Mrs. Field that she prepared a wonderful French meal complete with the finest wine. Ms. Boudreau's emails to her friend Lisa Bunt describe in detail the romance you and she were—"

"That's not true. We were not having a romance!"

"Don't interrupt me, Mr. MacDonald. You'll get your chance to speak. For now, just listen. You told me Ms. Boudreau never mentioned anything about her friends. Such a beautiful young woman would no doubt have many opportunities for relationships, so perhaps she chose not to tell you about them because you were the object of her desire. Ms. Boudreau was an incredibly beautiful woman and I would guess she was only twenty-one years old." The detective got up and moved beside David, placing a hand on his shoulder. "If a woman as beautiful and young as Ms. Boudreau was pursuing me, I would be somewhat flattered. It's not hard to imagine that after a fine dinner and a few glasses of wine you may have let things get out of control. After all, you're only human. Any man in your position would have done the—"

"I didn't do anything with Catherine."

"Mr. MacDonald, please let me finish. No doubt the affair seemed harmless enough until Ms. Boudreau told you she was pregnant." Richardson walked away from David, crossing the room. "I'm sure a man in your position would have used some sort of protection, unless of course she convinced you she was taking birth control pills. I understand you're a victim here, Mr. MacDonald. I'm on your side."

"Hold on a minute," David said. "Are you suggesting Catherine threatened me by saying she was pregnant, or are you actually saying she was pregnant?"

"She indeed was pregnant."

"Oh my God, I had no idea. But I am not the father of her baby, nor was I her victim in any blackmail attempt."

The detective swung his chair in front of David and sat again. "The evidence speaks for itself, Mr. MacDonald. You have no way out."

David leaned away from the detective. "I'm not guilty!"

"Okay. You insist on speaking rather than listening, so tell me why Catherine's bank account showed a deposit of ten thousand dollars from your business account. Was she blackmailing you, Mr. MacDonald?"

"No, she was not blackmailing me!"

"Then what was this money for?"

"I don't know anything about the money. I didn't write a check for ten thousand dollars or make a transfer of that amount to her."

"Are you suggesting she was stealing from the business account?"

"I wouldn't think so. I'm only saying I know nothing about the ten thousand dollars you're referring to. To the best of my knowledge, she would not have access to those funds, nor did she have any signing authority relating to the bank account."

"I want to believe you, Mr. MacDonald, but you're not helping me at all. Let me recap for you the mess we have here. You tell me there was nothing going on between you and Ms. Boudreau. Then we find out you have been to at least one romantic dinner with her, in her apartment. We have emails she sent to her friend Lisa Bunt describing a hot romance with you. We find pictures in your house of you and her in very suggestive poses. We know she was pregnant and ten thousand dollars showed up in her account from your business account. Yet you claim there was nothing between you and her. Having an affair is not a criminal offense, Mr. MacDonald. If you would simply admit to that, maybe we could find the truth about the other things. I hope you understand it's in your best interest to cooperate with us."

"I don't understand what is happening. I only know I'm not guilty of anything."

"Mr. MacDonald, I like you and I don't want to lock you up in jail. Help me to help you. Tell me what happened."

"I keep telling you, I don't know what happened to Catherine. I wasn't there."

"I don't want to lock you up, Mr. Macdonald. Jail is not a nice place. I'm going to go talk to my superior, and while I'm gone I want you to think about how you could help me to better understand what's going on. Give me something I can use to help you."

Richardson got up from his chair and walked out the door. David heard the click as the door locked behind him.

Richardson sat with his partner as they reviewed the case. Although there was ample evidence to suggest David had been having an affair with Catherine, nothing indicated he had killed her.

"I don't believe he's guilty, but we have nothing else to go on," Richardson said. "I'm going to let him sweat for a while, then see if he has anything more to say. Unless he has something to offer when I return, our next move is to get his DNA to see if he is the father of Ms. Boudreau's baby. If he is, he's been lying to me about the affair. If he's not, we have an additional person we need to be investigating."

———

As David sat in the interrogation room, he pondered all the evidence the detective had revealed. He knew it looked bad for him. He was so tired that he was void of all feeling.

He thought back to how he had lusted for Catherine. Even though he hadn't physically done anything, he recognized his guilt of lust and how that had opened the door for this mess. He searched his mind to try to find something he could put forth to prove his innocence, but there was nothing. He was terrified of the thought of being locked up in a cell.

He broke down and started to sob. He felt hopeless.

Suddenly, his thoughts came back to something Paul had once said: "When you're at the bottom of the pit and have no way out, look up to Jesus." David didn't even know what that meant, but he grasped at it and prayed.

If you are real, Jesus, help me!

David heard the unlocking of the door as Detective Richardson returned. "David, have you thought about how you can help us understand what's happening?"

"I don't understand it. I would help if I could, but I don't have any answers."

"Are you ready to admit you were having an affair with Ms. Boudreau?"

"I was not having an affair with her."

"David, admit the truth. Your wife will forgive you. It's not worth going to jail for."

"I was not having an affair with her."

"Give me something, David. I'm trying to help you."

"I've got nothing to give."

"If nothing else, you can give me one thing to help both of us."

"What's that?"

"You can agree to a DNA sampling. That will save me the paperwork required to get a warrant and I won't have to lock you up while we wait. Would you do that for me?"

"Yes. I just want to get this over with."

———

When David arrived home later that evening, Deborah could see he was totally wiped. Her heart broke as she felt the deep pain her husband was feeling. She wrestled between her desire to comfort him and the rage she felt over the likelihood that he had betrayed her.

Her deep love for him won out as she fought off her wrath and held him in her arms. David broke down and cried.

CHAPTER TWENTY

EDITH BICKLE FELT VIOLATED BY THE EXPERIENCE OF THE WARRANT being executed. It felt to her like the office had been burglarized. Desperately she tried to calm her nerves before her meeting with Mr. Cain.

During all the many years she had worked for Mr. MacDonald, she had never gone into his office without him being there. This tradition left her uncomfortable with now preparing to meet a client in his office. She pulled out his chair and unlocked his desk to retrieve the plan prepared for Mr. Cain. Nervously she laid everything out on the desk so it would be readily available for her presentation.

She went to check on the coffee and taste-tested it to assure its quality. Her nervousness caused her to regret she had ever agreed to do this. After all, Mr. MacDonald had given her the option to cancel the appointment and rebook it.

Her thoughts were interrupted when the office door opened and in walked a very distinguished-looking man.

"Mr. Cain, I presume?"

"Yes, but please call me Dennis. Is Catherine away sick or on vacation?"

"Unfortunately, I have bad news. Catherine passed away suddenly. That's why I'm here to help out until Mr. MacDonald recovers from the shock and can hire someone to replace her. My name is Ms. Edith Bickle." She hesitated for a moment, feeling the need to return his offer to use first names. "But please, call me Edith. I worked here for many years until my retirement and I came back to help Mr. MacDonald through this difficult time. I have all the information for your investment plan. If you're agreeable, I can go through it with you."

"I'm so sorry to hear about Catherine. Did you know her well?"

"I only knew Catherine for the weeks I trained her. Although I liked her, our age difference didn't leave us with much in common."

"Well, Ms. Bickle, you sound very competent. I'm sure you will do a great job going through my plan with me."

"May I get you a coffee before we start?"

"That would be wonderful. I take my coffee black."

There was something about Mr. Cain—no, Dennis—that made Edith relax. He was an extremely handsome man and was one of those people who seemed comfortable in his own skin. It made him so easy to be with.

As she reviewed the financial plan, he listened intently, asked great questions, and his smile somehow soothed her like no other smile had ever done before. She was smitten like a schoolgirl.

When Dennis complimented her on the clarity of her presentation and approved full implementation of the plan without even a single change, it pleased her to no end. Somehow through this process they had made such a connection that Dennis asked her out for dinner and she accepted.

Dennis had heard of people talking about finding a soulmate, but until meeting Edith he had never understood what they meant. He convinced her they shouldn't let the age difference get in the way of what could be a great friendship.

Edith persuaded herself there was nothing wrong with having a younger friend. In fact, it was probably a good thing.

That evening, as Edith got ready to go to dinner with Dennis, she cautioned herself to be realistic. This was not a date. He was many years her junior; they were simply two people who enjoyed each other's company. Nevertheless, she couldn't remember being so excited about going out to dinner with someone.

Dennis showed up at her door precisely on time. Edith was pleased with his punctuality, which was in her eyes an important characteristic.

When she opened the door, Dennis' greeting smile warmed her heart.

"You look lovely," he said.

Edith was somewhat embarrassed, for she had very little experience dealing with compliments from men. "Thank you. And you look very nice, too."

His car was exactly what she would have expected him to drive. Although her knowledge of cars was limited, she knew his Infinity was a pricey vehicle. It had a quiet elegance, was black in color, and was impeccably clean.

He held the door open for her. Inside, the luxurious leather seat wrapped soothingly around her. As Dennis walked around the car, she wondered what on earth she had done. Her nerves started to get the best of her.

Once they pulled away and Dennis started to converse again, the peace she had experienced during their first meeting returned. What was it about this man that made her so comfortable?

When Dennis pulled up to the restaurant, Edith's face lit up. "How did you know this was my favorite restaurant?"

"I didn't," replied Dennis. "I came here because it's my favorite and I hoped you would enjoy it, too."

They faced each other and laughed at this coincidence.

They entered the restaurant and the maître d' welcomed Dennis by name. He ushered them to a window table with a wonderful view. Edith felt so special.

They ordered drinks and the conversation eased into the getting-to-know-you phase. Dennis carefully and graciously explored why Edith had chosen to remain single. She told him that her family and upbringing had not set an example that made marriage attractive. There had been times when she regretted not having anyone close to share her life, but with the mess of the world perhaps not having others to worry about wasn't such a bad thing.

Endeavoring to steer the conversation away from herself, she asked Dennis if he had ever been married. Before he could answer, the waiter came to take their orders. Edith ordered the same meal she had enjoyed at this restaurant on previous occasions. The waiter smiled and asked if Mr. Cain would like his usual.

"Yes, Carl, thank you," Dennis said. "And would you refresh our drinks, please?"

"Certainly, Mr. Cain."

Edith was impressed that Dennis knew the waiter's name. She believed that taking time to know the names of people who served you in the course of business was truly the mark of a humble person.

Once the waiter left, Dennis responded to Edith's question. "No, I've never been married. Although I've been able to converse easily with you, that is usually not my experience with women. I have never had good luck with choosing girlfriends. I guess I've given up on ever finding anyone I can really trust."

Dennis went on to tell Edith he had never known his mother and had lived most of his life as a ward of the Child Welfare Agency. His story broke Edith's heart, for she knew something about the emptiness he lived with.

Just as Edith was saying she couldn't believe how much they had in common, the waiter served their dinners. He placed Edith's meal before her, then reached to the cart and served Dennis his meal. They all laughed when Edith saw that they had ordered the same meal.

"This is uncanny," she said.

"I know. When you ordered my favorite, right to having it cooked medium well, I couldn't believe my ears."

They laughed once again about the numerous things they had in common.

During the drive home, they sat in comfortable silence as Edith tried to figure out what would be the appropriate response to such a wonderful evening. Should she invite him into her apartment, or would that be too forward? She didn't want him to think she had romantic ideas. After all, he was half her age.

Dennis seemed to know what she was thinking. "Edith, I want to thank you for trusting that my intentions toward you are honorable. I know you had to move far outside your comfort zone to accept my invitation. As I told you, I've never known my mother and things never worked out with any of the foster parents I've had. I would very much like to see if we could develop a friendship that might fill a gap that I suspect is present in both our lives."

"I would welcome an opportunity to get to know you better," Edith said.

Dennis walked Edith to her apartment door and told her he would like to call her again.

"That would be fine," she replied.

He took out one of his business cards and wrote his personal cell phone number on it. "And please, any time you want to talk, feel free to call me."

When Edith went to put her key in the lock, they slipped from her fingers. Dennis was quick to bend over and retrieve them. While he was bent over, Edith noticed that he had a birthmark on the back of his neck. She was stunned to see that it was heart-shaped.

Dennis noticed a change on her face. "Are you all right?"

"I'm just not used to staying out so late. I'm feeling very tired."

Dennis unlocked the door, handed her the keys, and gave her a goodbye hug.

Edith stepped into her apartment and went directly to her computer. She clicked on Google and typed in: *How unique are birthmarks?*

CHAPTER TWENTY-ONE

DETECTIVE RICHARDSON OPENED THE ENVELOPE WITH THE DNA test results. The report found no match between Ms. Boudreau's baby and Mr. MacDonald, nor did the baby's DNA match to anyone on the Convicted Offenders Index—but a hair collected at the scene provided a match with another killing on the National Crime Scene Index. The same person had been present at the apartment of Ms. Boudreau and at the scene of the murder of a waitress by the name of Susan Oakley.

The detective realized this linked the two murders and provided credibility to the suspicion there was a serial killer on the loose.

Since the crime scene DNA didn't match the baby's DNA, there was obviously another person of interest tied to this investigation.

Richardson pondered his next moves. Although this added some credibility to Mr. MacDonald's statements, he and Mrs. Field were still the only leads he had. He needed to go back over their statements and ask them to come in to be interviewed again. Surely, they must have seen Ms. Boudreau with, or heard her talk about, another person. After all, no one could lead such a secluded life, especially someone as attractive as Ms. Boudreau. It was imperative to find other people who had known her.

He sent out officers to show the victim's picture in all the area bars, restaurants, and coffee shops. Someone must have seen her, and chances were good that someone so beautiful would be remembered. He then picked up the phone and called Mr. MacDonald.

The detective told David that his DNA proved he was not the father of Ms. Boudreau's baby, and this validated that there had to be another person of interest the police needed to interview. He asked David to come back into the station to be interviewed. They agreed on a time. The detective then called Mrs. Field and requested she return. She, too, agreed to meet with him.

———

David got off the phone and told Deborah the news.

"So the detective's done questioning you?" she asked him.

"I didn't get that impression from what he told me, but at least I'm back to being only person of interest and not the prime suspect."

"So where do we go from here?"

"So far as the police are concerned, I don't believe there's anything I can do other than to go through the process. I swear to you, Deborah, I didn't have an affair with Catherine, but I can understand how the pictures and the money transfer would make me look guilty. I don't understand what has happened, so I can't offer you any defense. Maybe Paul, with his experience, can help us get through this."

"You're right, David. We should call him. Go to your meeting with the detective and I'll see if I can set up a time for us to meet with Paul."

———

When Richardson ushered David into the interrogation room, he again reminded David that he was here of his own free will and could leave at any point. He was not being detained. David acknowledged that he understood.

"Think back to before the murder," Richardson began. "Did Catherine ever mention somewhere she went or anyone she went out with?"

"To the best of my recollection, she never mentioned anyone or told me anything about her social life."

"Did you ever notice anyone hanging around that for any reason made you feel uncomfortable?"

David thought about it and could only come up with one incident. He told the detective about the time when he and Catherine had been out for lunch and he had noticed a man following and watching them from the opposite side of the street.

"What restaurant had you been in?" asked the detective.

"Caplansky's Deli, down the street from my office."

"Is there anything else you can recall?"

"No, I'm afraid that's it. But I do have a question for you, if I may ask it?"

"What's your question?"

David went on to repeat that although he could understand that it looked like he had been having an affair with Catherine, it wasn't true. He had already gone after the bank to determine how the money transfer had been authorized and he felt sure they would eventually come up with an answer.

"Is there any place I could go to analyze the pictures, to see if they were Photoshopped?" David finally asked.

Richardson told David that he had sent the pictures to the OPP Forensic Center and that hadn't been able to prove beyond a reasonable doubt that the pictures were authentic. They forwarded the pictures to an expert at CSIS.

"I'll let you know when we get the report back," Richardson said.

David thanked him and asked if he had any further questions. The detective said no and thanked him for coming in.

———

Once David returned home, he found Deborah sitting in the den with a confused look on her face.

"What are you so deep in thought about?" David asked as he walked into the room.

"When I called Paul about counseling us, he agreed. But he asked me to first determine why I thought you were guilty of being unfaithful and what would have to happen for me to believe you're innocent." She patted the seat beside her to invite David to sit. "I realized that I intuitively knew the pictures weren't real. And if you were to transfer money to Catherine to pay off a bribe, you would have found a better way than what was done. So my main doubt is based on something other than the circumstantial evidence. The first time I saw Catherine, she looked like she had just walked off the pages of a glamour magazine. I realize now that I felt threatened by her. When the pictures were delivered, those feelings were resurrected."

Deborah took David's hand in hers and continued, her voice cracking. "As I gazed in shock at the pictures, the sight of Catherine's beautiful body made me feel like I couldn't compete with her. Why wouldn't you be attracted to her? It wasn't until Paul surprised me with his questions that I realized I had abandoned my trust in you because of my own insecurities. I jumped at the chance to place the blame for everything I was feeling on you. I'm so sorry!"

Tears formed in the corners of her eyes, then ran down her cheeks in an unbroken stream.

David took her in his arms and held her until her crying subsided. As he released her from his hug, he took her hand again. With tears forming in his own eyes, he thanked her for sharing her feelings with him.

"I believe that's one of the things we need to become better at in our marriage," he said. "I want to do my part by sharing my feelings with you. I too need to confess. My actions haven't been admirable since you became a Christian. I didn't realize until recently that I felt I was being replaced by your new love, Jesus. I was jealous and I, too, felt this great insecurity. You thought it was hard to compete with Catherine, but I felt I had to compete with God."

For the first time that day, Deborah smiled. "Yeah. I can see that may be a bit daunting."

"Yes. That is daunting, even for the great David MacDonald." His smile quickly disappeared. "First of all, let me tell you something. During all the years we've been married, I have never been unfaithful to you. I love you more and more each day. Prior to going to the marriage seminar, I sensed that your feelings for me had changed and you weren't as interested in me as you used to be. I know now it was my insecurity distorting my good sense. Whatever the case, it left me vulnerable to the attention I got from Catherine. Although I was never unfaithful to you, I did lust after Catherine in my mind, and I flirted in a way that may have led her on. So, to some extent, I'm responsible for much of what has happened, and I probably contributed to some of your feelings of insecurity. The only thing I can say in my own defense is that I didn't act on my temptations—and the moment I started to understand what was happening, I made sure Catherine understood how much I loved you and that there was no intention on my part for she and I to become more than friends. The marriage seminar revitalized my appreciation and love for you and for our marriage. Afterward, everything was going so well—and then everything blew up right in my face. I ask for your forgiveness for any pain my actions or thoughts caused you."

Once again Deborah had tears rolling down her cheeks. She wrapped her arms around David and told him how much she loved him. She asked him to forgive her for failing him in his hour of need. They stood and kissed, wrapped in each other's arms.

CHAPTER TWENTY-TWO

EDITH'S GOOGLE SEARCH DIDN'T TURN OUT AS SHE HAD HOPED. When she had noticed Dennis' birthmark, a memory she had buried deep down flooded back to her consciousness. She had barely been a teen when, as an unwed mother, she'd been sent to Guelph to have a baby. Her father had told the neighbors that she had gone away to care for an ailing aunt.

Once the baby was born, she had held it for only a short time before the nurses took it away, telling her it had a heart condition and needed special care. A few days later, they told her that her son had died.

Edith still remembered holding her son. She clearly recalled the heart-shaped birthmark on the back of his neck. Perhaps she was grasping at straws, but she had an eerie feeling that there was something more to the uncanny affection she had for Dennis. As crazy as it was, her maternal instinct cried out that he was her son.

She had hoped the uniqueness of the birthmark would further confirm her feelings, but she was disappointed to learn that many people had heart-shaped birthmarks. So many, in fact, that people with heart-shaped birthmarks compared experiences on line and many of them believed they had special sensitivities. One of those people had posted: "I have a heart-shaped birthmark on my left arm, which so happens to be my writing arm. I have always thought I was 'special,' as cliché as that sounds, but seriously! I know things before they happen. I have multiple déjà vu moments, I can feel what someone is feeling, what they're thinking. As weird as it sounds, I know a person's personality by touching them." There were many such postings.

Could that be why Dennis and she were so in tune with each other? Did Dennis have this special gifting? Could that be what made her feel such a strong bond with him? Were her feelings totally irrational? Was she letting her imagination run wild? No matter how unlikely the chances, Edith couldn't get over the feeling that Dennis was her son.

When she got to work the next day, she pulled Dennis' file and looked at the copy of his birth certificate. He had been born in Guelph on exactly the same day Edith had given birth!

She didn't know what to do. After a life of living without any family, would Dennis even want to know his mother? If he did, she didn't want to build up his expectations and then find out she had been a fool for trusting her instincts. That would grieve him and damage their relationship.

Suddenly, she went to the computer and searched for private DNA-testing companies in Toronto. She found a company near her home and copied the list of what was needed in order to have a DNA test performed. She planned how she might obtain the required samples at a barbecue Dennis had invited her to at his home.

———

Once again, they had a wonderful time together. Dennis prepared a succulent steak, something similar to scalloped potatoes, and a wonderful serving of mixed vegetables.

They enjoyed a fine wine and good conversation. Edith carefully moved the conversation to exploring if Dennis had ever tried to find his birth parents. He indicated he had, but the records from the hospital had been destroyed in a fire so he couldn't go any further.

Satisfied that he would want to find his birth parents, she felt a little better about what she had done while he'd run out to pick up some spice he had been missing.

When she got home, she was rather proud of her detective work. She had taken some samples of hair from his hairbrush, a paper cup he had used from the picnic table, and a bag of garbage from his driveway. She hoped to obtain a few more useable items from the garbage bag contents.

She spread an old blanket out on her kitchen floor and shook out the contents of the garbage bag. As she started to sift through the garbage, she came across a number of photographs that had been torn apart. Immediately she recognized part of David Mac-Donald's face. As she looked closer, she pieced together pictures of David, Deborah, and several of Catherine. It troubled her that some of these pictures showed the subjects in the nude. What had Dennis been doing with these pictures, and how had he obtained them?

Edith also found a magazine with individual letters cut out on different pages. She remembered how one of the detectives executing the search warrant had received word that nude pictures of the victim had been found.

Could this have anything to do with the trouble Mr. MacDonald was having? Edith became very worried about what she had found and felt guilty about having taken it from Dennis' driveway. Her dishonesty, together with the thought that she may have found a son nobody knew she had, wove a web so tight that there was no way to reach out to anyone for guidance.

Anyone, that was, except Dennis himself.

CHAPTER TWENTY-THREE

DENNIS AWAKENED WITH A NEW JOY IN HIS HEART. LIFE HAD SEEMED so much better since he had met Edith. He lay in bed trying to figure out what it was about this woman that was so unique. He knew there was no sexual attraction, as she was very much his senior, yet there was something. Maybe the age difference was the main factor. He had never explored a friendship with a woman for any reason other than physical attraction. Perhaps he was filling the tremendous emptiness he felt from not having ever experienced a mother's love. He feared, however, that Edith may turn out to be another woman who ended up disappointing him. It scared him to let his mind travel down that road, but he knew he had to take the risk.

He hopped out of bed, turned on the coffee maker, and reached out the front door to get the paper. As he flipped through the pages, he noticed an extensive article on Catherine's killing and a picture of her. The police were asking for anyone who had known her to contact them. The article went on to reveal some of details of her death. The one that caught Dennis's eye was that she had been in the early stages of pregnancy and that the fetus had been too young to survive. Dennis read that sentence over and over again. His stomach turned as he realized he was responsible for taking the life of a child.

Women like Catherine were a cancer in his life, and the only way to survive them was to cut them out—but the child had been innocent. He sat at the table and cried over the death of this child. He felt a pain inside his spirit he had never felt before. The pain became worse as he realized there was no way to undo what he had done.

The real perpetrator was the man who had impregnated Catherine without having made a commitment. Was that man Mr. MacDonald? The father deserved to pay the penalty for his action, and Dennis vowed to do everything in his power to make sure justice prevailed.

CHAPTER TWENTY-FOUR

Diary Entry, June 16, 2013

Thought of the day: What looks like trouble is really faith on its way to greatness.

As I ponder Deborah, my meeting with Paul, and all that has happened to me in the last while, I wonder if this quote can be true. I know my life has been changed by what has occurred. In some ways, these events will make me a better person. I have now committed my life to Jesus, and that alone will have a dramatic effect on me.

Deborah and I, in spite of what's happened, are in a better relationship than ever. Through it all, I've realized that any control one believes they have over life is an illusion. No matter who you are, how careful you are, and how well you've planned, everything can change at the drop of a hat.

Paul nailed the solution to all this when he said that if there is no God, then life is like the ball in a pinball machine as it bounces from one place to another with no particular purpose. The alternative points to a God who declares that we do have a purpose and that He loves us. We're still not in control, but He is the one pushing the buttons on the side of the pinball machine.

Each flip of a lever directs our trek to make it purposeful. Each event is an opportunity for growth.

If there isn't a life after this world, life truly sucks. If, however, there is purpose to the happenings in this life, we should want to receive the benefits.

The question is, how? Jesus has said to believe in Him, for He is the way. He knew many wouldn't believe Him, so He issued his challenge: "Try me and see that I taste good." In today's terms, the equivalent statement is "The proof is in the pudding."

Jesus claims that trusting fully in Him and following His ways won't just get you to the next life, it will also give you the power to overcome this life. You will be able to rise above your circumstances. This doesn't suggest that you won't have problems in this world, though, for He has said, "In this world you will have trouble. But take heart! I have overcome the world."

I don't fully understand all this myself, but I've decided to taste and see if He is good. So far, His ways have helped me rise above my circumstances. As I learn more about His teachings, everything makes more sense.

I'm heading back to work for the first time since all hell broke loose. I must admit that I've lost my previous confidence that if I lived right, everything would fall into place. That scares me.

———

As DAVID ENTERED THE BUILDING, HE SENSED TENSION. PEOPLE seemed to avoid him, and those who did greet him gave no opportunity for conversation as they quickly walked by.

When he reached his office, Edith asked him if he had read the morning paper. He replied that he hadn't, so she showed him that the article called Catherine "the mysterious one." The police had been unable to locate anyone who had known her other than her employer at Star Investments. Edith had received several calls from clients questioning the events relating to Catherine's murder and contemplating closing their accounts.

Although this somewhat hurt David's feelings, he wasn't surprised. Investors were a nervous bunch and they reacted unkindly to uncertainty. People tended to believe the worst of others.

We all know our shortcomings, David thought. *Given the chance, we want to pull others down to our perceived level.*

David returned the investors' calls and had some success convincing them to trust him and hang in until the case was solved. There were, however, those who wouldn't listen.

Afterward, he felt it was only fair for Edith to be privy to the whole story as he knew it. He asked her to come into his office and he told her everything. She showed her true colors; like Paul, she had no hesitation in believing that David couldn't be a party to the crime.

As she heard this new information, Edith decided to wait for the DNA results before she confessed to Dennis what she had done. If she told him what David had just told her, it could trigger Dennis to say something about his involvement without her needing to ask.

David asked Edith to close up, as he was exhausted from his first day back and wanted to leave early. She was happy to oblige.

Once he arrived home, David poured himself a glass of wine and sat down to try to calm himself. He wondered when this nightmare was going to end.

CHAPTER TWENTY-FIVE

As Edith prepared to close the office, she received a phone call from Dennis inviting her to dinner on the weekend. Edith cheerfully accepted.

When he asked her how her day had gone, she took advantage of his question, hoping to get him talking about his involvement with David's case—hoping to hear any clue to explain the pictures she had found in his garbage.

She told Dennis it had been a difficult day and recounted how several clients had read between the lines of the newspaper story that David, being one of the few people who knew Catherine, must be a primary suspect in her murder. She told him David was a good man and that there was no way he could have been having an affair with Catherine.

At the end of her story, Edith waited for Dennis to reveal something, but he said nothing. They talked a little longer, made plans for a future dinner, and then exchanged goodbyes.

———

Dennis contemplated what Edith had told him. Most of what she'd shared wasn't news to him, except for the fact that the DNA proved David wasn't the father of Catherine's baby, nor was David a match for the DNA found on Catherine's bed. That DNA—Dennis' own DNA—matched what had been found at another crime scene.

He was confused about David not being the father of Catherine's baby. Dennis thought he'd known everything about Catherine, but obviously she had been involved with someone he knew nothing about. He trusted Edith's opinion of David and conceded he could have been wrong about David and Catherine having an affair. For Edith's sake, he decided to give David a little help by sending a helpful report back to the OPP regarding the pictures they had sent him for authentication. He could say those pictures, in his professional opinion, had been doctored.

———

When Edith arrived home, she was excited to see that she'd received mail from the DNA testing company. She nervously opened the envelope and couldn't believe her eyes. The report indicated that Dennis was indeed her child. The report went on to say that due to an unusually high sharing of DNA chunks, she should come in to meet with one of their genetic counselors. Further DNA testing of other family members may be required to explain this phenomenon.

The service was expensive, so Edith thought this could be a marketing ploy to get her to overspend. She decided to do some research on her own to better understand the results before booking another meeting with the company.

She found out that DNA is the carrier of our genetic information and is passed down from generation to generation. All of the cells in our bodies, except for red blood cells, contain a copy of our DNA. At conception, people receive DNA from both the father and mother. Each person has twenty-three pairs of chromosomes, and of each pair, one is received from the father and one from the mother. These pairs are known as nuclear DNA, because they reside in the nucleus of every cell in the body. The twenty-third chromosome is known as the sex chromosome—as with the other chromosomes, one is inherited from the father and one from the mother. The mother's chromosome is always an X, and the father's can be either an X or a Y. Therefore, the father's chromosome determines the gender. XX chromosomes are female and XY chromosomes are male.

The use of DNA had become big business in family tree research, since it could determine a person's major population group and provide information about their ancient origin. Analyzing children's DNA to diagnose developmental disabilities and congenital anomalies had also become more prevalent. Her attention was particularly drawn to a statement that said extensive DNA testing had major ethical, legal, and social implications; a genome showing an absence of heterozygosity, reflecting that large chunks of the mother's and father's contribution were identical, pointed to incest.

After reading this, Edith knew she had to spend the extra money. She certainly couldn't approach Dennis until she fully understood what this information meant.

CHAPTER TWENTY-SIX

Diary Entry, June 20, 2013

Thought of the day: You are armed and dangerous! Your tongue is a dangerous weapon that when unleashed is deadly; gossip is a cowardly way to fight a war.

The events of the last few days have certainly made me realize how true these words are. Many people have been crucified by innuendoes and half-truths. Irresponsible words are being printed and spoken to such an extent that it's becoming the norm. Politicians ruthlessly use this form of warfare against their opponents, and although the public expresses their dislike of such campaigns, their votes don't always express the same condemnation. It's no wonder people don't trust authority figures.

In our world, we are bombarded with lies. Where would you go to seek truth?

As a new Christian I find it particularly interesting that Jesus said, "I am the way and the truth and the life. No one comes to the Father except through me."[2] Even thousands of year ago, it would appear that He realized our need for a source of truth.

———

IT WAS TIME FOR DAVID TO HEAD OFF TO WORK, BUT HIS HEART WASN'T in it. The events of the past few days had caused him to question what the point of it all was. Life was so fragile and it seemed there was no way to protect oneself. He felt totally vulnerable.

As he pulled into the office parking lot, he was horrified to realize he had driven the whole way so distracted that he couldn't remember the trip.

Edith greeted him as he came through the door and handed him his coffee and messages. He immediately thought of how Catherine had always gone into his office and left everything on his desk. Catherine had always been so cheerful.

He suddenly realized he hadn't really grieved his loss of such a good friend.

The horrible events he had lived through were like a bad dream. Everything had happened so fast there had been no time to think, no time to feel. All his efforts had been directed toward survival, like a man flailing, trying to keep his head above water.

Now that the end was in sight, he was tired and depressed. He threw himself into his work to ignore the pain.

Later that morning, his phone rang. It was Paul, who wondered if David wanted to grab a quick lunch with him. David was delighted; the timing of the call couldn't have been better. Paul was one of those people who could lift his spirits simply by being there. He always knew what to say. More importantly, he was a good listener.

David quickly accepted the invitation and they decided to meet at the deli down the street from David's office. As David arrived at the deli, he saw Paul waving from a corner table. They greeted each other, left their coats at the table, and went to select their lunch. They both ordered corned beef sandwiches.

Back at the table, they turned their full attention to the savory treat, engaging in typical small talk between bites.

Once they finished and sat back to relax and enjoy their drinks, David mentioned that this was the same place he and Catherine had gone for lunch on her first day.

"I'm having a difficult time putting this all behind me," David confided. "I know trouble is supposed to make us stronger, but I certainly can't say I feel stronger right now."

Paul moved his plate to one side. "Sometimes the best we can do in a day is simply get through it. It will take time to process everything you've gone through. Be patient, David."

"Yeah, I know you're right, but patience isn't one of my virtues. I want things to go back to where they were before this all happened. Back to when I was sitting on top of the world."

"I don't blame you for a minute," said Paul. "But it's been my experience that we can never stay at the top of the mountain. Sooner or later, gravity takes over and down we come. This isn't necessarily a bad thing, since most often we fall to a plateau which is higher than where we sprung from. When we restart our climb, we can climb higher than we've ever been before, stay longer, and enjoy it more. Life is a process. Right choices spiral us upward and bad choices drag us down."

"Quite frankly, I don't even know which way I'm heading."

"We know our choices are leading us in the wrong direction when we need to lower our standards in order to match them," Paul said. "You know you haven't lowered your standards, David. In fact, you've raised them, so trust the process. Good things are coming."

"Thanks, Paul. I needed a pep talk. This one will help me to hang in until better things start to happen in my life."

"If you were to come over to my garage and help me work on the Chevy, I bet that would lift your spirits even higher. I've got some serious work to do tonight."

"Sounds like a bit of a con job to me, but I'll be glad to help."

"See you at 7:30?"

"You're on."

David said goodbye and walked away feeling better than he had all day.

CHAPTER TWENTY-SEVEN

EDITH'S FOLLOW-UP APPOINTMENT WAS DEVASTATING. SHE WAS TOLD that the unusually high sharing of DNA chunks between her and her son's DNA indicated there had been an occurrence of incest within her family in this current generation.

Embarrassed, she didn't know how to react. "Are you sure?"

"We've given you the best information we have," the counselor said. "You'll have to decide what you do with it. If you so desire, and the relatives are still alive, we could do more testing to clarify the situation."

Edith wanted to get out of the meeting and absorb what she had been told. She told the counselor she would think about it and decide if she wanted to proceed further. She hurried out of the office with tears flowing down her cheeks.

She drove home in a daze, the news echoing in her mind. Once she arrived, she went directly to her couch and lay down, exhausted from all she'd been through. Sleep eventually overtook her.

Her dream world brought her back to when she had been a teenage girl hurrying home from school; she had stayed later than usual and knew her dad would be furious with her being late. Suddenly, a man jumped from the alley, grabbed her, and pulled her behind a large garbage bin. Although he wore a hood, she remembered his haunting eyes. The man got up after raping her and pulled off his hood.

She woke up in a sweat, screaming.

For the first time ever, she was embarrassed to be part of her family. This wasn't the heritage she wanted to pass on to her son. Would she ever be able to tell Dennis she was his mother? Questions raced through her mind, one after the other, but the most fearful one of all was how Dennis would react. Would he want anything to do with her knowing all these details? Maybe the most loving thing to do was to let the relationship come to an end so he would never know where he had come from. So he would never know the awful truth.

The more she thought, the more confused she became about what to do. She needed to confide in someone and decided to ask her former psychologist, and current minister, Rev. Paul Evans if he would help her sort through this mess. But how would she even face him?

CHAPTER TWENTY-EIGHT

WHEN DETECTIVE RICHARDSON INTRODUCED HIMSELF ON THE phone, David's heartrate raced.

What now? he thought. But to his surprise, the detective opened with the words, "I have some good news for you."

David felt a wave of relief flow though his body. "You don't know how much I need some good news for a change. Go ahead, I'm all ears."

"I have received the test results performed by CSIS and they state that the pictures were doctored, created by someone with outstanding ability. Therefore, they are no longer relevant evidence so far as my investigation is concerned."

"Thank you so much," replied David. "That is, in fact, great news."

Armed with this new information, David was ready to take on the company he had hired to do the sweep. After all, they had failed to find evidence that his house had been bugged. He looked up the number and called, asking to speak to the manager. He was put through to Mr. Salter. David explained what had happened and asked how it could be that no evidence of any bugging had been found.

Mr. Salter put David on hold while he searched for his file. After a long wait, he told David that he had no record of any service personnel being dispatched to Mr. MacDonald's home. There was no invoice issued, nor payment received. David asked what their service vehicles looked like. The manager told him they were bright red with the company logo and name on the side. David realized he had been duped. He thanked the manager for his help and hung up.

The only way this made sense was if the man who'd come to do the sweep had been the same one responsible for invading his privacy in the first place. This man had pulled off some very slick maneuverings to carry all this out.

But he made one big mistake.

CHAPTER TWENTY-NINE

EDITH CALLED REV. EVANS AND ASKED IF HE WOULD MEET WITH HER. She confided that she had been raped and had never before discussed it with anyone. Hearing the pain and fear in Edith's voice, the reverend asked if she would be more comfortable with him coming to her place. Edith gratefully accepted this offer. She didn't want to run into anyone, at church or elsewhere, with tears in her eyes. The last thing she needed was for her friends to start asking questions she didn't want to answer.

She prepared tea and searched her mind for how to tell him her story.

When her doorbell rang, she almost hit the ceiling. Her resolve to put on a strong front was lost the minute she opened the front door. Tears flooded down her cheeks as Rev. Evans took her hand in his.

"Edith, I know it was extremely difficult for you to ask me here and I thank you for trusting me."

He released her hand and she led him to the living room where they could sit and talk. Edith sat on the end of the couch and Rev. Evans sat on the chair nearest her.

"I don't know where to start," Edith said.

"You told me on the phone you had been raped. Tell me what you can about it."

Edith told him the story about how it had happened. She had wanted to keep the rape from her father, but then she had realized she was pregnant and would soon start to show. Back in those days, abortion hadn't been an option, so she'd had no alternative but to tell her father. He had been furious with her and said her pregnancy would tarnish their family's good name. He had sent her away to have the baby and told the neighbors she was away helping an ailing aunt.

She'd had a beautiful baby boy but only got to hold him once for a very few minutes. The nurse took him away and later told her he had died.

"Much to my father's delight, I went home emptyhanded," she finished. "Although I grieved the loss of my child, none of this was ever discussed again."

"You've never mentioned anything about your mother," Rev. Evans said in a soft voice. "What happened to her?"

"My mother died while giving birth to me, and I've always felt my father blamed me for her death. He was always angry with me no matter how much I tried to please him."

"You've carried this immense burden on your shoulders all your life, but now you've let it out and can begin to heal. None of what you've told me is your fault. You are the victim! Your father made an awful mistake in blaming you." Rev. Evans came over and sat beside Edith, took her hands into his, and prayed, "Lord, you have empowered Edith to finally share this burden she has been carrying for so long. Help her now to rely on You so she can lay down this burden You never wanted her to carry in the first place. Help her to find Your peace, Lord. Free her from any chains the evil one has confined her in. This we pray in Jesus' name." He opened his eyes and smiled at her. "Edith you've taken a courageous step by being willing to tell your story. No doubt this has been very tiring for you. I would normally suggest we break so you can rest, but I sense there's more to your story and now is the time for you to get it all out."

"You're right. The story only gets worse. Are you sure you want to hear it?"

"Yes, Edith. I want you to release everything that has a hold on you. Now is the time."

Edith sat up very straight, with a look of determination painting her face. "Okay, here it goes. When I came back to work for Mr. MacDonald, he asked me to meet with a new client. From the first time I lay eyes on him, I was smitten. Although he was many years my junior, I felt something for him that I couldn't understand. He obviously had similar feelings, because he asked me out for dinner. I'm appalled to say that I accepted.

"We had a wonderful time and got together on other occasions later. One evening when he was dropping me off at home, I dropped my keys and he bent over to pick them up. As he did this, I noticed the birthmark on the back of his neck—it was the same as the one on my baby. Together with the feelings we had for each other, this started me thinking that he might be my son. I checked his records at work and found he had been born in Guelph, which was where I had my baby, on the same day of the same year. I decided to obtain some samples I could use to have his DNA tested, to see if there was a match to mine. Knowing he desired to be part of a family, I didn't want to raise his hopes until I knew for sure.

"When the test results came back, they identified him as my son. This made me incredibly happy, but there were some irregularities that worried me, so I had another meeting with the company that had done the testing."

Edith proceeded to tell him what they had revealed to her. She looked up at him to see if he was disgusted with her story. To her surprise, she saw compassion in his eyes.

"Go on," he told her. "It's important to get this all out."

"The problem now is that I don't know what to do."

Edith broke down and cried uncontrollably. The reverend placed his arm over her shoulder and told her to let it all out. They sat together for a long time, until Edith finally began to stop crying.

"Would it be better for Dennis if he never knew the truth? That would mean he'll never know I'm his mother, and that would break my heart. But what would it do to him to know he came from such a family? Dennis is a very successful man. He works for CSIS and I suspect he may even have helped the local police on Mr. MacDonald's case. Would such a man want to know he had such a horrible family history? I don't know what to do."

"When one doesn't know what to do," Rev. Evans said, "it is always a good idea to see what the Bible has to say about their situation. Your question boils down to this: should you tell the truth or withhold it? The Bible's answer is that the truth will set you free. You have unloaded a lot of baggage, and I'm sure during the next few days you will feel a burden has been lifted. Don't let yourself fall into the trap of again going down the road of burying the truth."

"I understand, but I'm so afraid of what might happen."

"Trust in the Lord, Edith. He won't let you down."

They decided to stop there and give Edith time to recover from the ordeal of telling her story. They made plans to meet again in a few days and closed the meeting in prayer.

As Rev. Evans headed for the door, he turned to Edith. "What were you referring to when you mentioned that your son Dennis may have helped with the case?"

Edith told him about the torn pictures she had found in his garbage and that she hadn't asked about his involvement because it would require admitting to stealing DNA samples.

"Fortunately, Mr. MacDonald told me the other day that CSIS was asked to check the authenticity of the pictures," she said. "That explains why Dennis had them."

Rev. Evans again praised Edith for her courage. He hugged her and then said goodbye.

CHAPTER THIRTY

ALTHOUGH DENNIS WAS LOOKING FORWARD TO DINING WITH EDITH, he couldn't shake the horror he felt over the death of Catherine's baby. This child had been an innocent victim. He wracked his brain to understand how he could have been so wrong about Catherine and David. Could he possibly have been wrong about other things also? His feelings for Edith had caused him to regret the actions he had taken in his prior relationships. Maybe he had been too quick to judge. Maybe the penalty for his prior lovers' indiscretions had been too severe. His relationship with Edith had changed everything; although he loved being with her, his life was falling apart.

He had a great new joy, and at the same time this profound sadness. Was he losing his mind? He started to wonder if Edith was another of the cancers women brought into his life. Did he need to cut her out?

As he pondered these thoughts, his phone startled him. It was Edith, asking him if they could change their dinner plans. Instead of going out, she wondered if he would consider coming to her place to have a home-cooked dinner. She had some serious things to talk with him about.

Dennis agreed to the change of plan but was very uncomfortable.

Later that night, he arrived at Edith's with a bottle of wine and some beautiful flowers.

Edith thanked him and put the flowers in a vase on the dining room table. She asked him if he would pour them both a glass of wine as she put the finishing touch on dinner. They sipped on their wine and conversed about the weather and current news.

Dennis became impatient. "Edith, what did you want to talk about?"

Edith sat with her hands in her lap, twiddling her thumbs. "When you thought about finding your birthparents, did you ever consider how you would feel if they turned out to be less than what you hoped for?"

"What do you mean?"

"Well, for instance, what if they were drug addicts or alcoholics who lived on the streets? Would you still want to find them?"

"I never really got that far. As I told you, my records had been destroyed in a fire. Why are you asking this? Do you know something about my birthparents?"

"Yes, I do. But I don't know if you're going to like what I have to tell you. If you prefer, we can leave it all unsaid."

Dennis' mouth fell open and tears filled his eyes. "You're my mother, aren't you?"

"Yes, I am."

"Oh my God, I can't believe this! I somehow knew it, but I can't believe it. That's why I had such strong feelings for you from the day I met you."

He moved towards Edith as a teardrop filled his eye, dragging with it an army of tears to wash away all the loneliness and hurt he had carried. Edith took him into her arms as they both wept uncontrollably. They remained locked in each other's arms for what seemed a lifetime, making up for all the lost years.

"You need to know the whole story," Edith said when finally they separated.

"I don't care what you did or who you were. You don't need to explain anything to me. I already know I love you more than anyone I've ever known." With that, the tears flowed and they embraced again. "I love you so much, Mom."

"I love you too, son."

The joy of using those words flowed through them. The feeling of being loved and having roots was overwhelming.

Edith backed away. "Let me at least assure you I never willingly abandoned you. I was a teenager when I had you and I was told you died of a heart complication. I suspect this was my father's doing so he wouldn't have to deal with the complications and embarrassment of his daughter having a baby. I should have known because he sent me away to have the baby but no arrangements were ever made to deal with what happened afterward. I only got to hold you once, right after you were born, and then they took you away. My heart broke and I never stopped grieving for you. Many a night I fell asleep crying, wishing you had lived. I prayed to God that I would be with you when I reached heaven."

"No need to say more, Mother. In the short time I've known you, I've come to see you are a kind and loving person; you would never have abandoned me. We no longer need to grieve. Now we are together and can make up for lost time." He hesitated before going on. "I sense there are complications surrounding my birth that are difficult for you to talk about, and perhaps difficult for me to hear. I would prefer, for both our sakes, to leave all that in the past and focus on what we can have now."

"That may be a good idea," replied Edith.

They sat on the couch holding hands and looking at each other with a sense of awe at this amazing turn of events.

Suddenly Edith exclaimed, "I have a great idea. Dennis, you suggested we should go from this day forward, not looking back, so why don't we plan a party to celebrate the birth of our relationship? It will be our first family tradition, one we will celebrate from this point forward. I can invite all my friends and show off my son. You can invite your friends, too."

Dennis' countenance fell. "I really don't have any close friends to invite."

Edith smiled. "Don't worry, son. I know my friends will love you as much as I do, and they will be friends to you as they have been to me. You already know Mr. MacDonald, and I'm anxious for you to meet Rev. Evans. He is such a nice man. I'm sure you will like him."

"Okay, but only if you let me help prepare and host the party. I don't want you doing all the work yourself."

"You're such a thoughtful son," said Edith. "Now let's have our cold dinner and plan our party."

The dinner and planning went on for hours, and by the end they were both worn out. As the hour was late, Dennis readied to go home. He kissed Edith goodbye and went out to his car.

His mind reeled on the drive home. After all these years he had a mother—or did he? He heard a voice in his mind echoing over and over: *She will never love you, baby killer.*

Dennis had never felt such angst. The thought of once again losing his mother was more than he could bear! Once his mother no longer loved him, he would be right back where he had come from: an abandoned child. He couldn't let that happen.

CHAPTER THIRTY-ONE

Diary Entry, July 17, 2013

Thought of the day: Life is infinitely stranger than anything which the mind of man could invent. There are dramas unfolding all around us that we don't see or we choose not to see.

Perhaps today will provide some new clues as to who tried to set me up for Catherine's murder. Detective Richardson has agreed to send someone over to dust the telephone relay box, and Mr. Salter will be by today to perform a sweep of all the electronic and communication equipment in the house. If he doesn't find any bugs, he'll look for evidence that bugs may have been there but have since been removed. Although fingerprinting the telephone relay box is a long shot, Richardson said it's usually the long shots that break a case wide open.

I have a feeling that I'm finally closing in on who has been messing with my life—and perhaps even the person who killed Catherine.

I've prayed that God would help me find the person responsible for Catherine's death, and I feel that He is in the process of answering my prayer.

I'm going to shower and get my day going. I'm eager to put my plan into action.

Mr. Salter pulled into the driveway in a bright red van. The emblem on the truck had a fisherman's net over the company name: Security Net.

David went out to meet him and tagged along as he did his work. No current bugs of any kind were found, but Mr. Salter did locate pinholes and scratches in places unlikely to have been damaged by day to day activities. The most telling piece of evidence was found in the attic, where it looked like cameras had been set up. Care was taken to not contaminate the scene so David could have Detective Richardson confirm the findings.

Although, none of this new information identified a specific perpetrator, David was hopeful this effort would produce new leads.

Soon after Mr. Salter left, a forensic officer showed up to check out the phone box. Once he finished, he informed David that Detective Richardson would be in touch with him. David thanked him and watched as he drove away.

According to Richardson, the telephone company's records showed that only two repair employees had been sent to David's relay box in the last year. They had both agreed to provide their fingerprints, thereby allowing the police to identify if any unauthorized individuals had tampered with the box.

David was enthusiastic about the possibilities and eagerly awaited Detective Richardson's next call.

CHAPTER THIRTY-TWO

WHEN THE DAY OF THE PARTY CAME, DENNIS WAS SO EXCITED THAT he left his home at ten o'clock in the morning. He decided to take the subway rather than his car. This would provide additional needed parking at Edith's house for the guests and allow him to drink without worrying about having to drive home.

He and Edith worked well getting things ready for the party and they had a lot of fun doing it. At the end of the day, they felt well-prepared to host the party.

As the hour approached, Dennis got more and more nervous about meeting Edith's friends. What would they think of him? Would they love him like she'd said they would? Would they accept him as Edith's son?

The doorbell interrupted his thoughts and he heard Edith welcoming the first of the guests.

"Dennis, you know Mr. MacDonald," Edith said when Dennis entered. "And this is his wife, Deborah."

Dennis reached out a hand to Deborah. "Please to meet you, Mrs. MacDonald."

"Please, call me Deborah," she said.

"Thank you for coming to our celebration," Dennis said. "Come in and sit down. Help yourselves to a drink from the table we've set up in the corner."

Dennis ushered them into the living room and over to the table. As they each fixed their own drinks, Dennis asked Deborah if she worked outside the home. She smiled and said that she worked for the provincial government. Dennis wondered why she didn't just say she was a judge.

"And what exactly do you do?" Dennis asked, probing deeper.

"Well, I'm a judge. I try to not tell people, because there's often a tendency to react poorly."

"I understand where you're coming from," said Dennis. "I get the same type of reaction when I tell someone I work for CSIS. They seem to feel like I'm going to check out all the details of their lives. The truth be known, my workday is mostly consumed working on the computer and it can be rather mundane. Nothing like the 007 image one might bring to mind."

"Let me be the proud mother and tell you his job is much more interesting than he's letting on," Edith piped in. "He's a data exploitation analyst. When we hear that someone with bad intentions has been stopped from planting bombs and such, it's because someone like Dennis discovered their plans."

"Wow!" said Deborah. "That sounds exciting."

"It's a rare situation," Dennis said. "More often than not, we spend day after day analyzing information and end up with absolutely nothing."

"No matter," said Deborah. "I can see why you're proud of your son, Edith."

Edith was about to say something when the doorbell rang again and she went to answer it.

As the evening went on, more and more of her friends came in. Dennis loved the attention he was getting. He had never even had a birthday party, and this was the party to make up for it. Edith's friends loved him, just as she'd said they would. They were all lovely people. Dennis was surprised at how easily he fit into this group and his role as her son.

He was pleasantly surprised when the people he had invited from work, and his fellow volunteers from Big Brother, showed up.

He had never thought of them as friends; in fact, he never thought he had any friends.

As Dennis mingled with the guests, he became aware of Mr. MacDonald looking at him and then away as soon as he glanced back in his direction. It made Dennis uncomfortable, but he brushed it off and focused on enjoying the moment.

Throughout the evening, Paul also noticed David's continuous glances at Dennis.

"What were those looks all about?" Paul asked once they had a little privacy.

David was appalled that he had been so distracted as to be evident. "I'm sorry, Paul. I hope others don't interpret it as boredom with the party. I certainly don't want to give that impression. It's just that I suddenly feel like I know Dennis from someplace apart from work, but I can't remember where. It keeps eluding me."

"The mind can be a wonderful thing. Eventually you'll figure it out," Paul said. "Put it aside for now. Let's go have a drink and get back to the party."

"Isn't it amazing?" Deborah said when they were on their way home. "After all these years, Edith finally has the child she always wanted. It's like her dead baby coming back to life. He seems to be a remarkable man and he has beautiful, haunting eyes."

"That's it!" said David. "It's his eyes. They are exactly the same as the man who came to check out the house for bugs. How coincidental is it that he's also a data exploitation analyst?"

"What are you saying, David? Do you believe he's the man who came to our house?"

"I don't know, but there's some connection. I can feel it in my bones."

"Now that you mention it, I'm getting my own eerie feeling. I didn't remember before, but there was a man in my courtroom during my last case. I felt like he had penetrating eyes, and I can see the same quality in Dennis."

———

First thing in the morning, David called Paul to tell him about what he and Deborah had sensed.

"I don't want to falsely accuse anyone," David said, "but I suspect Dennis may be the man who did the fake sweep of my house."

As Paul listened to David, he thought back to what Edith had told him about the photos in Dennis' garbage. He felt torn between keeping Edith's confidence and sharing the information with David. Paul bought himself time to think by putting off the discussion until they could meet together.

CHAPTER THIRTY-THREE

When Dennis woke up after spending the night of the party at Edith's place, he could smell bacon cooking. He lay in bed thinking about the incredible party they had hosted and the wonderful time he'd had.

Edith's friends had all been so accepting of him—all, that is, except for David. All night long Dennis had felt David's eyes peering at him. He felt threatened by what David may have somehow figured out. He knew if others found out the truth about him, he would lose everything, including Edith's love. He couldn't let that happen.

No sooner had he put aside this worry than once again a haunting voice echoed in his head: *Baby killer.*

He jumped from bed to escape the torment of his mind and sought relief in the cleansing water of the shower. When he stepped from the shower, he felt better. He dressed and went down the stairs in response to the beckoning bacon.

"Good morning sleepy head," Edith said. "How are you doing this fine morning?"

"I'm wonderful and I'm hungry."

"Good. Eat well, because you'll need lots of strength to help me clean up the mess left behind from last night's party."

Dennis hugged her. "Thank you again for the wonderful party."

"It was for both of us, so don't you be trying to get out of the cleanup by calling it your party."

Dennis laughed. "Well, I tried."

One part of Dennis enjoyed his breakfast conversation with Edith while another track looked for a solution to the problem David presented.

"I'm so glad you agreed to stay over last night," Edith said. "We both needed to rest before tackling this cleanup job. And there's something important I want to talk to you about. Why don't we take our coffee into the porch where we can sit and chat?"

"Did I do something wrong?"

"No. I want to speak with you so I don't do something wrong, something I would regret forever."

"This sounds serious."

"It is," replied Edith.

They each grabbed their coffee and headed for the porch. The porch was bright with the early morning sun and a pleasant breeze blew through the screened windows. The well-padded wicker furniture and view of the backyard gardens made this an ideal place to sit and enjoy coffee.

"So what is it that's so important?" Dennis asked once they were settled.

Edith's face took on a serious expression. "When you were born, the circumstances were such I couldn't prevent the evil that was going to befall you. Now I have the opportunity to help save you from an even greater evil and I don't want to fail you again. So listen very carefully to what I have to say. I suspect from our previous conversations that you are not a Christian, am I right?"

Dennis frowned. "I haven't told you much about my childhood. I didn't want to cause you grief, but I sense the time has come to tell you some of my story."

Edith took his hand. "Please do."

"As a young boy, I hoped someone would adopt me and that life in a family would be better than what I was experiencing. But as time went by, it never happened and I lost all hope. When I was twelve, a church provided the opportunity for a few children from our home to go to a summer camp. I couldn't believe my good fortune. I was one of the ones picked to go. I had the time of my life! I got to ride horses, paddle a canoe, and play games. It was wonderful. During the two weeks I was there, I heard about Jesus for the first time. They told me that God loved me and wanted me to join His family. Can you imagine what that meant to me?"

Edith squeezed his hand. "So what happened next?"

"I went up to the front and said I wanted Jesus to be my Savior. They led me in what they called the sinner's prayer."

"Do you remember anything about what was in the prayer?"

"Yes. I was to give up my life to Jesus so He could clean me of all my sins and help me to change my ways. To me, that was a really good deal because my life wasn't worth anything as it was."

"Then what happened?"

"The camp ended and I went home. Although I prayed to Jesus, nothing seemed to change and eventually I lost all hope. That's my story, Mother. Now you tell me: am I a Christian?"

Edith smiled. "Have you ever heard the story of Moses?"

"Yes, I have," replied Dennis. "In fact, I've seen the movie."

"In the story, God tells His people that He'll use Moses to gain their freedom from slavery and bring them to a Promised Land," Edith said. "This was the answer to all their prayers. The slavery symbolized sin and Moses foreshadowed Christ. Forty years after God first told them He would free them, they finally found themselves in the Promised Land. And here you sit today. After all these years, you have a mother who loves you and that makes you part of a family. Even though you gave up on Jesus, He never gave up on you. He always keeps His word. So I guess the question is not whether you're a Christian but whether you'll respond to Jesus' faithfulness to complete what He started so many years ago?"

Dennis looked at Edith lovingly. "I've felt loved ever since I met you, and my life began to change. Finding each other was indeed miraculous, perhaps even an answer to my prayers many years ago. That gives me new hope. Perhaps Jesus loves me in spite of my many sins. But I must ask, if He does love me so much, where was He when I was suffering in my childhood?"

A tear rolled down Edith's cheek. "He was suffering for you on the cross so your circumstances and sins need not define who you are. Let me assure you, Jesus does love you, no matter what you've done. He is your only means of salvation. I started this conversation by saying I didn't want to fail you again, and that's so important to me because the consequences of not receiving Jesus as savior are enormous. People don't want to contemplate hell. No matter how you try to avoid reality by putting up smokescreens, the truth is the truth and the cost of being wrong is much greater than you will want to pay—especially when you consider that Jesus has already provided all you need. Following Jesus is a win-win situation. You have everything to gain and nothing to lose. You already trusted in Him to be your savior once. I now ask you to recommit your trust in Him and agree to make an effort to understand and live following His ways. Do you want to do that?"

"Yes, I do."

"Then, son, pray this prayer with me." Edith took his hand in hers, bowed her head, and prayed, "Lord Jesus, I know I am a sinner. I believe You died for my sins. Right now, I turn from my sins and open the door of my heart and life. I receive You as my personal Lord and Savior. Thank You for saving me."

Edith stood up, still holding his hand. He stood to meet her in an embrace.

She wrapped her arms tightly around Dennis. "Welcome, son, to the family of God. I'm so happy you have taken this step. I want us to meet with Rev. Evans so you can learn more about Jesus and get to a place where you're ready to be baptized."

Edith and Dennis cleaned the house and then had a light lunch. Dennis kissed his mother goodbye and left to head for home.

As Dennis stood waiting for the arrival of the subway, he looked at a mother and baby standing near him. The same accusing words echoed in his mind: *Baby killer!* As he fought to control his thinking, two young teens chasing each other around accidentally hit the stroller and sent the baby flying down into the track area.

Before he even thought about what he was doing, Dennis jumped down, grabbed the baby, and lifted it up to its mother. As the mother grabbed the baby Dennis, heard a voice speak to him: *A life for a life, a baby for a baby. You are forgiven.*

CHAPTER THIRTY-FOUR

Diary Entry, July 20, 2013

Thought of the day: When you paint yourself into a corner by fearlessly following the call of God, rejoice for there is nowhere else to go but up!

Yesterday as I walked in the park, I saw a grandpa with his granddaughter. He was watching her fearlessly climb a slide. She was only about a year and a half and climbed to the top of the slide with much effort and determination. Without any hesitation, she hurled herself down the slide and immediately started the climb again. She did this time after time, enjoying the fruit of her labor, when suddenly she fell off the slide platform. It was quite a tumble, but she quickly stood up and said, "Oh! Oh!" And then went right back to climb the slide again.

As I move along my new walk with God, I realize that needs to be my new outlook: to fearlessly pursue the life God wants me to live. When I fall (fail), I should say "Oh! Oh!" and then get up, dust myself off, and go right back to accomplishing what God has given me to do. No wonder Jesus tells us to be child-like.

———

DAVID WAS EAGER TO PURSUE HIS SUSPICIONS ABOUT DENNIS, BUT HE didn't know where to start. He called Detective Richardson and asked if they had found anything new from the forensic information they'd gathered. The detective told him that the forensics department had found a set of prints and a DNA sample from a wire inside the telephone relay box that didn't match the telephone company employees. This suggested some unauthorized person had worked on the box. Although this was helpful, it wouldn't be of value unless the police could match the samples to a specific person—and so far the police didn't have a suspect.

"If you had a suspect, could you require them to provide a DNA sample?" David asked.

"No," the detective replied. "Not unless there was solid proof that the suspect was involved in a violent offense. Even then, a judge would have to grant the authority to require the sample. Why? Do you have someone in mind?"

"Yes, but I have nothing to substantiate my suspicion other than a gut feeling."

"Who do you suspect?"

"His name is Dennis Cain and he works for CSIS."

Richardson remembered the name from the report regarding the pictures. "I'll look into this new information. Thank you for calling, but I should warn you: be careful about playing detective. It could end up being dangerous."

"I have no plans to play detective," David assured him. "That's why I called."

"That's good. I'll let you know if anything new comes up."

They exchanged their goodbyes and David hung up the phone.

David left the house to meet Paul for coffee. He told Paul all about the talk he'd had with the detective. Paul didn't want to share the information he had learned from Edith. But he, too, was now suspicious of Dennis. He feared Dennis had set David up, and perhaps even killed Catherine. Was Dennis really Edith's son, or had he managed to fake that, too?

"Earth to Paul," David called out.

"Sorry. My mind was somewhere else. What are you planning to do now?"

"I don't believe there's anything I can do except follow the advice of a very wise man who once told me that when you don't know what to do, pray and ask God."

"Indeed, that fellow was a wise man," Paul said. They both laughed. "Speaking of God, how is your spiritual walk going, David?"

"It's going well, but I'm struggling with the idea that Jesus is the only way. It's not a problem for me personally, but I look at people who are Muslim or any other religion that doesn't accept Christ as savior, and somehow it doesn't seem right that they give their whole lives to what they believe and yet according to Christianity they are lost."

"It's not a new problem," Paul said. "When Jesus was here on earth, he said to his followers, 'Just as the living Father sent me and I live because of the Father, so the one who feeds on me will live because of me.'[3] The disciples had a hard time accepting that, and many left him because of it."

"So what's the answer?" asked David.

"This question has been addressed in various ways, but to me it simply comes down to this: on your own, you have no way to get to God. Go ahead, right now. Go to God. You're still here, David. Why don't you go?

"I see your point. I can't go to God."

"Nor can I or anyone else take you or send you," said Paul. "Jesus is Emanuel, which means 'God with us.' God came to earth to get us. He did what was required by dying on the cross so that we could be saved. He's the only one who can bring us

---

3 John 6:57

out of this world and into the next. Why would anyone believe anything different?

"To better understand, consider a crime that's punishable by death. Only the person with the highest authority in the land is authorized to commute the sentence. The Bible tells us that the penalty for sin is death and that we are all sinners. Therefore, we are all condemned. As Jesus is God, He is the highest authority. He is the one who must declare us pardoned. That's the prime difference between Christianity and all other religions. The others attempt to avoid the sentence on their own terms, but Christianity proclaims the terms set by God.

"There's an account that says President Andrew Jackson is the only president to have one of his pardons rejected. George Wilson, a postal clerk, had robbed a federal train and killed a guard during Jackson's presidency. The court had convicted him and sentenced him to death. Because of public sentiment against capital punishment, Jackson granted Wilson a pardon. But Wilson refused it! The Supreme Court had to step in to decide if a person could refuse a presidential pardon, and it decided that a person is free to decline a pardon. In other words, a person must actually accept the pardon. Similarly, salvation is available to *all* through Jesus, but they must accept it."

"Well, that makes sense to me," David said. "If we desire to enter a new universe once we die, we need to comply with the authority of that universe."

"You're right, David. The very first story in the Bible tells us about Adam and Eve. They lived with God in the garden He created for their pleasure, and they could remain with Him in that perfect environment, but there was a condition: they were not to eat of the fruit of the tree of knowledge of good and evil, lest they die. This proclamation is significant because it asks a question: do you believe God or do you think you know better? They chose to follow their own way, and as a consequence they were kicked out of the garden. God gives each person this same opportunity. He says to each of us, 'The way to Me is through Jesus.' That's the condition, and we either accept it or we're left on our own. In my vast counseling experience, I've found there are many reasons for the troubles people have, but by far the greatest is that they refuse to follow God's law. To those who proclaim they don't need God, I wish with all my heart that they would ask themselves, how's that working out?"

CHAPTER THIRTY-FIVE

AFTER DENNIS HAD LEFT FOR HOME, EDITH SAT DOWN TO PRAISE God for all He had done in her life. Their party had been a wonderful way to celebrate the gift of her son. She thought about the Bible story where the father of the prodigal son put on a feast when his son finally returned home. How well she understood how that father felt. She wished she could reach out to someone who was aching for the deliverance of one of their children, to tell them not to give up and keep praying.

Our God is indeed a mighty God, she thought.

Her thoughts were interrupted when the telephone rang. She answered cheerfully, expecting it to be her son.

"I'm calling from St. Michael's Hospital," the voice on the other end said. "Do you have a son named Dennis Cain?"

Edith's face grew somber. Worry flooded her body. "Yes, I do."

"We have admitted a man and his identification indicates he is Dennis Cain. We were unable to find any contact information in his belongings, but he had your number on his phone."

"Is he all right?" asked Edith.

"He is in critical care. You should get here as soon as possible. When you arrive, the doctor can fill you in on the details of his condition."

Edith's voice cracked as tears filled her eyes. "I'm on my way."

She hung up and phoned Rev. Evans, who agreed to meet her at the hospital. She grabbed her keys and was out of the door like a shot.

Functioning on pure adrenaline, she weaved through traffic. Even though she went as fast as possible, it seemed to take forever to get there. She ran from the parking lot toward the hospital until shortness of breath forced her to slow down. At the reception area, she asked for directions to her son's room. It annoyed her that everyone was casual in their responses.

Upon entering the room, she saw a body wrapped in bandages that looked like a mummy. Could this possibly be her son? Perhaps there was some mistake?

The nurse sitting by the bed asked if she was family and Edith replied that she was Dennis Cain's mother.

"Is this him?" Edith asked.

"That's the identification he had on him." Seeing that Edith was starting to sway, the nurse quickly reached out to catch her. Edith fell gently to the floor.

When she came to, the nurse was holding her head tilted back on the floor. She tried to get up, but the nurse restrained her and told her to stay put for a few minutes.

Once her senses cleared, Edith realized that Rev. Evans had arrived and was by her side. He and the nurse helped her sit up on the chair by the bed.

The doctor soon arrived. He already knew the reverend and directed him and Edith to a small lounge outside the room. He told them that the patient had been hit by a subway train while saving the life of a baby.

"Is my son going to live?" Edith asked.

"We've done everything we can and now only time will tell," the doctor said. "The next few hours will be critical."

The nurse entered the room and motioned to the doctor. The doctor told Edith and Paul to stay where they were and that he would be back as soon as he could.

Paul reached out and held Edith's hands.

"Before leaving this morning, Dennis accepted Jesus as his savior," Edith said.

"God is good, Edith. Let's pray."

When the doctor returned, his face was solemn. "I'm so sorry to tell you that your son has passed away."

Paul opened his arms to Edith as she buried her head against his chest, sobbing heavily as she repeated the words "Why, Lord? Why, why, why?"

Paul didn't say anything. He simply held her and cried along with her.

When Paul and Edith walked to the nursing station to find out what needed to be done, they were told that because of the condition of the body no certain identification had been made. This needed to be completed before the body could be released.

"Do you know his dentist?" the nurse asked Edith. "Where did he live? Where did he work?"

Edith answered their questions, but she didn't know who his dentist was. She advised them that his DNA was on file. They took her information.

"As soon as the identity is confirmed," the nurse said, "we'll let you know and the body will be released."

Paul asked Edith if she would allow him to handle the communications with the coroner and she readily agreed. He also insisted that Edith let him drive her home. He would arrange later to get her car back to her place. Edith was in such a state of shock that she complied without any argument.

Paul drove Edith home and got her settled in. He made her a cup of tea.

Edith felt cheated that she'd had so little time with her son. She was thankful God had used her to bring her son to a saving relationship with Jesus, but she was still angry that he had been taken away so soon.

Paul wanted to arrange for someone from the church to stay with Edith overnight, but Edith declined the offer. She needed some time by herself to work through all that had happened.

"I'm going to take care of picking up your car," Paul said. "I'll check on you when I return. If you need anything, my cell number is on this card. Don't hesitate to call me."

With that, he left Edith alone with her thoughts.

CHAPTER THIRTY-SIX

THE COMBINATION FROM THE FORCE OF IMPACT AND THE BURNS Dennis received from the track made facial recognition impossible. The coroner didn't use the DNA on file, as there was no way to prove the sample had been taken from Dennis Cain. The CSIS Human Resource Department was contacted and able to identify his dentist. Dennis Cain's dental records proved a positive match to those of the victim. The majority of the fingerprints taken from Dennis Cain's home matched the prints taken from the body. The coroner was satisfied the body was that of Dennis Cain, so he signed the death certificate and advised Paul that the body could be released.

Part of the process of identifying an unknown corpse was to run the DNA and fingerprints against the Convicted Offenders Index and the National Crime Scene Index. This resulted in Detective Richardson being advised that the DNA linked Dennis Cain to three of the young women who had been murdered. The fingerprints also matched those put on file from the telephone box at David MacDonald's home. This proved that Dennis had been present at each of the crime scenes and that he had tampered with David's phone.

The coroner finally released the body and Edith, with Paul's help, began to make funeral arrangements.

CHAPTER THIRTY-SEVEN

"To start, Dennis' mother Edith has asked me to share some of their history so we can better understand the difficulties her son had to overcome in order to have a successful life," Paul said, opening the funeral service. "Dennis was separated from his mother at birth. His mother was told he had died, but in fact he had been placed into the care of the Child Welfare Agency and grew up in group homes. Throughout this time, he never knew the love of a mother or father. Somehow, through all the problems he encountered, he achieved prominence as an agent for CSIS and was well respected by his peers. He was active with Big Brother Big Sister and mentored several boys. It was only a short time ago that fate brought Edith and Dennis together, and they found great love as mother and child. Before I go on, I want to open the service to anyone who would care to share something of their relationship with Dennis."

Several minutes passed before a short, dark-skinned man came forward. "My name is Tony. It's hard for me to come up here because my English is not so good. But I wanted to say how good Mr. Cain was to me and my family. The first year I was in this country, I got a job as a security guard with CSIS. Being new to the country, we did not have very much money.

"The very first time Mr. Cain came through the gate, he asked me my name and spoke to me like a friend. Each day he asked me more about my family. A few weeks before Christmas, he asked me if I would let him buy my son a Christmas present because he loved children and he didn't have anyone to buy for. I suspected he was trying to make it easy for me to accept his charity. I'm a proud man, but his gentle manner made it easy for me to accept. I almost cried in front of him when he came in a few days before Christmas with a trunk full of gifts for my son. I went home and piled them under the tree. My wife and I thanked God for providing this man to bless our son.

"On Christmas morning, my son opened present after present. We were shocked when he got to the end and brought the last two presents over to us.

"'These are for you,' he said.

"Mr. Cain gave me the wonderful watch I'm wearing today, and he gave my wife a beautiful set of earrings and a matching necklace. That's the wonderful kind of man he was and I will miss him very much."

Another person came forward and took the microphone. She was the past president of Big Brother Big Sister and recounted how Dennis had set up a fundraising campaign to provide the opportunity for some of the little brothers to go to camp. The first year, he had sent five children to camp. Last year, the number had grown to twenty. He had been a tireless worker when it came to the welfare of children.

Next, a lady came up and told her story. She was a working single parent. Her teenage son was more than she could handle and had been headed for serious trouble, flunking out of school. In desperation, she contacted Big Brother to see if they could help. That was when Dennis came on the scene.

"I don't know how he accomplished what he did," the lady said, "but I know that my son eventually came to love him. He was the father the boy never had. Dennis was always there when needed. My boy is now in university, on his way to becoming a medical doctor. All his university costs have been paid for by Mr. Cain. I wouldn't want to imagine where my son would have ended up if it hadn't been for him."

Paul thanked those who had told their stories and asked a woman named Maria Thompson to come forward. She approached the front of the church holding a beautiful baby boy.

"This is the baby Dennis saved and his mother Maria," Paul said, handing the microphone to Maria.

"How does a mother begin to thank someone who saved the life of her child?" Maria said. "How do I stand in front of a grieving mother who lost her son in order that I keep mine? Nothing I could say or do would be adequate. I make this commitment to you, Ms. Bickle. I will do everything in my power to raise my child to be someone your son would have been proud of. I also want you to share in his upbringing as an honorary grandmother. I know this won't replace your son, but in some little way it may help."

Maria walked over to Edith. Both had tears streaming down their cheeks. Edith stood and embraced Maria and the baby.

Paul moved to the microphone and began to speak. "John 15:13 says, 'Greater love has no one than this: to lay down one's life for one's friends.' When we come together to celebrate a life, we're trying to discover who the person was. Did his life matter? My wish is that this service will lead each of you to ask yourself how you will be defined. You are not defined by your past, your present, or even your future. You are not what you do, and you're not what others define you to be. You're not the sum of your activities. However, little is said about how you should define yourself. Why do we have such a difficult time defining who we are? It strikes me that if we're not defined by our past, present, or future, maybe we're defined by the choices we make along the way.

"Serious card players will readily tell you that it's not the hand you're dealt, but rather the way you play it out. Life bears this out. It would seem the difficulty in defining who we are is that we haven't yet arrived. New lives are being created by God every day, but these are not found in the birth of children. They are found in the hearts that turn to Jesus. Who you are will be determined when you are brought before the Lord Jesus to be judged. His word will be the final word. No other opinions count. Jesus himself said, 'I am the way and the truth and the life. No one comes to the Father except through me.'[4]

"Edith told me that before Dennis died, he accepted Jesus as his Savior and Lord. She has peace in her heart knowing that Dennis is in a much better place. How about you? Are you at peace? Do you know who you are? Perhaps a better question is this: do you know Whose you are?"

The service ended and the guests were invited to join Edith in the church hall for refreshments.

David mingled with the guests, waiting for a chance to catch Paul alone. When he got his chance, he asked Paul if they could meet for breakfast in the morning. David needed to discuss the unsettled feeling the funeral had left in him.

---

4 John 14:6

CHAPTER THIRTY-EIGHT

PAUL AND DAVID ORDERED THEIR BREAKFAST. ONCE THE WAITRESS left, Paul asked David what it was that had upset him about the funeral.

David hesitated. "I hope this won't sound horrible, but I was angry at all the praise given to Dennis by the people who went up to speak. You heard enough from me to know I strongly suspect Dennis killed Catherine and tried to frame me. His funeral seemed so unfair to Catherine's memory. She was a good person who was kind to everyone she met. She didn't deserve what was done to her, yet when we arranged her burial the only people there were you, me, and our spouses. To make matters worse, Dennis is supposedly forgiven by God because he prayed the sinner's prayer. Where is the justice for Catherine?"

Paul set his elbows on the table with his fingers interwoven under his chin. "There are times, David, when we don't understand God's ways. King David committed adultery with Bathsheba and then murdered her husband to cover up what he had done. He eventually confessed his sin to God and God forgave him. However, God says that although he was forgiven, the consequence of his sin was that King David's son would soon die. This reveals that forgiven sin may still have consequences. So what does it mean to be forgiven? In this case, God maintained a relationship with King David, but he suffered terrible consequences for his sin."

Paul stopped speaking while the waitress served their breakfast.

"You asked the question, where is the justice for Catherine?" Paul continued once the waitress had left. "Let me ask you this: what would you consider to be just?"

David was shaking salt on his breakfast, probably more vigorously than he realized. "Justice would be that he went to jail—or better yet, was executed!"

"And if he had been jailed or executed, what difference would it make?"

"It would make me feel better," David replied angrily.

"So is it justice or revenge you seek?"

"I don't know," David growled. "Let's just eat our breakfast."

They ate their breakfast without any further words crossing the table. When they were nearly done, the waitress came by and asked if they would like more coffee. They pushed their cups forward.

Once she left, David took a sip. "Sorry, Paul, this has made me so angry. I'm having a hard time dealing with it."

"It's okay. You're angry because you sense an injustice and that is a characteristic you inherited from God. God is just. The problem is that we don't really understand what justice is and we don't understand God's ways. When Jesus was hanging on the cross, breathing His last breath, He said 'Father, forgive them, for they do not know what they are doing.'[5] Never forget that we live in a world heavily influenced by Satan. As Christians, we are told that we are to be at war against evil, not the people who are trapped by evil.

"Every time we don't do what God would have us do, we sin— and sin always has consequences. Sin is against God, and God alone, but the consequences of sin flood the earth and can jump from person to person, from generation to generation. It's much too complex for us to judge, but God tells us that the world will eventually see His justice and mercy in action and we will be in

---

5 Luke 23:34

awe of it. So, David, I say to you: trust in God for the justice you're looking for. Be kind and merciful, for how we judge others is how we will be judged."

"Thank you, Paul, for once again giving me wise advice," David said. "And I think it's only just that I pay for breakfast."

"That certainly sounds just to me," replied Paul as they both broke out laughing.

As David drove home, he noticed a religious billboard that read "There's more hope for murderers than there is for the self-righteous." That just about stopped him in his tracks.

———

What does that message do for you?

I invite you to visit www.god4.ca to share your reading experience and further explore some of the topics brought to light in *Thistle Hill*.

DISCUSSION QUESTIONS

In the court case Deborah presided over, the term ageism is defined as the stereotyping of and discrimination against individuals or groups because of their age. The plaintiff's lawyer, Mr. Baker, goes on to say, "The greatest danger of discrimination of any kind is that when the lies are repeated often enough, the victims themselves start believing the stereotyping used to discriminate against them."

- Describe any evidence of ageism you have encountered or observed.
- Aging, like any type of growth, involves change. What is your greatest fear about aging?

During the marriage conference David and Deborah attended, the instructor gave this definition for love: "Love is choosing to want the betterment of another to such an extent that you are willing to give up of yourself in charity for that purpose."

- How do you feel about this definition?
- Unconditional love is a charitable gift from the giver and requires nothing of you. Would you desire to be loved that way? Do you believe you would be capable of loving that way?

Remember the sign posted at the marriage conference, which read, "Don't even think about how today's subject material applies to your spouse or anyone else; focus on how it applies to you." David decided he should aspire to be the best person he could be, regardless of how other people responded to his changes.

- Discuss how you would feel if you continued to strive for the betterment of someone and they were not thankful for your efforts.

All of the characters in the book except for Deborah grew up missing the love of one or both parents.

- What impact do you believe this has on a person's life?
- Might it be a factor in what these characters are searching for throughout their lives?

When Dennis and Edith meet, there's an attraction between them that makes no sense to either of them. The story attributes this to Edith's maternal instinct.

- Do you see this as being realistic?
- How much of a factor would you suspect genes and upbringing play in determining who a person is?
- Had Dennis lived longer, do you think he would have changed and come to understand the gravity of the murders he committed?

Paul believes there are moral laws that when broken unleash consequences into the world. These consequences may affect not only the perpetrator, but any number of other people. They can jump from generation to generation and may follow the perpetrator to the afterlife.

- Do you believe your individual choices are that impactful?

Paul asked, "What is justice, and how does it differ from revenge?"

- Discuss situations you've heard about, or perhaps even encountered, where someone put their own life at risk to right an injustice.
- How does this compare to what you've encountered when you've observed revenge in action?

The book started with David contemplating his purpose in life.

- How would you respond to his question?

ACKNOWLEDGEMENTS

In this book, I reference God's words: "The two become one." When a Christian married couple experiences the significance of this truth, they realize that nothing either spouse accomplishes is done independent from the other. In marriage, both partners can remain fully who they are yet live in a harmony of oneness with each other. This all happens when they are married under God's covenant and the power of authentic love is at work.

I acknowledge my wife's tremendous contribution not only in the writing of this book but also to the writing of the story of who I am in Christ. Her example was the beacon that turned me to Jesus. I love you and thank you for putting up with me, for loving me at my worst and for always standing by me.

A huge thanks to the prayer group God selected to empower me throughout this process—Arlene, Bud, Dale, Dave and June, Debra, Garry and Twyla, Helen, Jane, Jef, Lori, Patricia, Peter and Eileen. The book was written on the wings of their prayers.

A big thank you to my friend and confidant Ansue, who played such a vital role in encouraging and supporting me throughout this process. I look forward to the day when I will be holding his book in my hands.

Thanks to my son Rob for his encouragement and computer expertise; to Merv, who sat through many a breakfast-get-together discussing *Thistle Hill* with me; to Dan, for contributing to the story; and to Norm, for getting me started.

The ultimate thanks goes to God for allowing me to take part in what He will do through this book and the God^4 series.

I also want to thank and bless you, the reader. My prayer for you is from Numbers 6:24–26: *"The Lord bless you and keep you; the Lord make his face shine on you and be gracious to you; the Lord turn his face toward you and give you peace."*

ABOUT THE AUTHOR

We are who Jesus says we are. Therefore, I cannot tell you who I am, but I can witness about my life in Christ. At the time of this writing, I am closing in on my seventieth birthday and I am still excited about where God will lead me next.

I identify with the Bible character Caleb, who at the age of eighty-five wholeheartedly wanted to claim all God had for him even though he knew there would be giants to overcome before he got the prize. I don't believe this was a sign of bravery on his part; rather, it reflected the strength of his faith in God.

When God led me to start writing *Thistle Hill*, it was so far out of my comfort zone that I had difficulty to believe I was receiving the correct message. After much arguing with God, I finally conceded and set to work. *Thistle Hill* is the evidence of faith put into action. Praise be to God!

My wife Pat and I live in Barrie, Ontario and have been blessed with a blended family of three children, six grandchildren, and two great-grandchildren. Our faith in God has led us to a place where we can start each day optimistic about what God has planned for us. We are mature enough to realize that the road God will lead us down isn't always the one we would choose. But experience has proven that it's always the road that is best for us.

My hope is that *Thistle Hill* will convey that God loves *you* and is eager to have a relationship with you. All you need to do is accept His offer.